SELECTING THE WRONG LOVE

THE LOVEWADE TALE SERIES
BOOK ONE

E. MASSON

JULIE G. HENRY

CONTENTS

This is a work of fiction — vii
Publisher's Note — ix
Acknowledgments — xiii
Selecting The Wrong Love — xv

Prologue — 1
1. Destined to Collide — 5
2. Where Our Stories Meet — 9
3. The Quiet Current — 13
4. Shadows of Tomorrow — 17
5. Hearts on Hold — 21
6. The Spark of Change — 25
7. A Choice between Hearts — 29
8. Shattered Bonds — 33
9. Broken and Unraveling — 37
10. Awakening Desire — 41
11. When Life Changes Course — 45
12. The Weight of Sacrifice — 49
13. Fractures in the Silence — 53
14. Love in the Cold — 57
15. Behind Closed Doors — 61
16. Haunted by Desire — 65
17. The Weight of Secrets — 69
18. Irrevocable Consequences — 73
19. The Choice Unveiled — 75
20. Echoes of Betrayal — 79
21. When Love Isn't Enough — 83
22. When Love Runs Out — 87
23. Hearts in Transition — 91
24. Resilience in the Ruins — 95

25. Shelter in the Storm	99
26. A Mother's Welcome	103
27. When Hope Returns	107
28. A Chance to Shine	111
29. The Strength Within	115
30. Fierce in the Fire	117
31. Roots of Hope	121
32. Amber's Little Entrepreneur	125
33. Dreams after Dark	129
34. Can't Stop Thinking about You	133
35. A Deal for the Future	137
36. A Step Too Late	141
About the Authors E. Masson and Julie G. Henry	149
Also by E. Masson and Julie G. Henry	151
A Note From the Author	153

Selecting The Wrong Love
(Book 1 of the LoveWade Tale Series)
ISBN: 979-8-9905474-7-6

COPYRIGHT © 2025 BY E. MASSON & JULIE G. HENRY

ALL RIGHTS RESERVED

All rights reserved. This publication, or the parts thereof, may not be reproduced in any form, stored in or introduced into a retrieval system, or transmitted, in any form, or by any means, electronic, mechanical photocopying, recording or otherwise without the prior written permission of the copyright owner of this book.

THIS IS A WORK OF FICTION

Names, characters, places, and incidents either are the product of the author's imagination or are used fictitiously. Any resemblance to actual persons, living or dead, businesses, establishments, events, or locales is entirely coincidental.

PUBLISHER'S NOTE

IF YOU PURCHASED THIS BOOK WITHOUT A COVER, BE AWARE THAT IT IS STOLEN PROPERTY. IT WAS REPORTED AS "UNSOLD AND DESTROYED" TO THE PUBLISHER, AND NEITHER THE AUTHOR NOR THE PUBLISHER HAS RECEIVED ANY PAYMENT FOR THIS "STRIPPED BOOK."

DEDICATED TO OUR BEAUTIFUL FAMILY

You all are the light that brightens our days and the inspiration behind every word written in these pages.

Your laughter and kindness fill our hearts with joy and give our pen wings to fly.

You have magic in you that's opened our eyes to the endless possibilities that await us on the journey of life.

Thank you for being our greatest treasure and constant source of love.

With all our love!
E. Masson & Julie G. Henry

ACKNOWLEDGMENTS

We would like to express our deepest gratitude to all the readers who've been on this literary journey with us.

Your support, encouragement, and enthusiasm have been the driving force behind the creation of this book.

Thank you for investing your time in the imaginary world within these pages.

Your passion and willingness to dive into each of our new adventures inspires us to continue writing and exploring new places and emotions.

We're immensely grateful for your feedback, reviews, and words of encouragement.

They've motivated us to push our creative boundaries and strive for excellence in every chapter.

This book is written for each and every one of you.

All of you believe in the power of words to transport us to magical places, ignite our imagination, and touch our hearts. So, we hope we'll continue this journey filled with wonder, discovery, and endless inspiration together.

With heartfelt appreciation,
E. Masson & Julie G. Henry

SELECTING THE WRONG LOVE
(BOOK 1 OF THE LOVEWADE TALE)

It's time to transcend reality!

Grab a cup of tea or coffee.

Relax, there's adventure ahead!

PROLOGUE

Amber let the soothing motion carry her thoughts far beyond the garden as she sat on the porch swing. She imagined herself as a doctor, wearing a white coat with her name stitched on it, and a stethoscope resting around her neck, ready to help anyone who needed her. Pulled back into reality, Amber took another look at the acceptance letter she had received three days back, and the world outside her garden appeared uncertain.

Every time Amber faced hardships, she grew stronger, and today was no exception, as her life was about to change in a considerable way. Raised by her mother, Linda Phil, from the age of five, after a fatal car crash took her father's life, they made a tiny home out of love and practically nothing else. Yet, it always felt warm.

Amber walked into the house knowing that saying

goodbye to her mother would be really tough. Her voice shook as she said, "Mom… I'm nervous. Being away from you feels awful."

Linda pulled her into a comforting hug and replied, "I'll miss you more than words can say, but you can do this."

"You've always believed in me; that is how I know I will be the best doctor I can be."

"You're special," her mother said, her voice heavy with love and sadness.

From the outside, you might not call Amber a genius, but at school, she always brought home top grades, and their small town could never offer the opportunities she needed.

Linda couldn't help but see Amber differently. When Amber told her that she always put her on a pedestal, all she could do was to show Amber that she genuinely cared.

Linda gently held Amber's face and looked into her eyes with conviction, as she told her to never forget that she was special and that she would always be loved.

Comforted, Amber smiled back, certain that love would be the constant she carried with her wherever she went.

Although she was initially reluctant to send her daughter away to Eryden University, Amber's years of hard work, studying, volunteering, and searching for new horizons had paid off in the form of a full scholarship.

The day the acceptance letter arrived was filled with tears and tight embraces. Mother and daughter celebrated Amber's future together, knowing they were stepping into a journey that would only make them stronger.

The final weeks passed in an emotional blur. Now, Amber stood beside her suitcase in the driveway, waiting to leave. Her final hug from her mother brought them both close to tears. She said, "I'll do enough good as a doctor for both of us, Mom. I promise," and exhaled a breath of hope. Her mom, though struggling to stop her tears, didn't doubt her one bit. "Remember, this will always be your home. I'll be here for you."

Amber took one final look back, waved at her house, and got into a taxi that would take her to the city and Eryden University. "Here I go." She summoned all the courage she had to face her new life.

CHAPTER 1
DESTINED TO COLLIDE

The imposing buildings and sea of students made Amber feel impossibly small when she started at Eryden University. Coming from a small high school, she was no stranger to feeling lost, and on her first day of orientation, that fear pressed in hard.

Her cautious smile worked as an effective mask for the anxiety simmering beneath it. Her heart pounded, caught between excitement and intimidation. She clutched her campus map, scanning it for landmarks, only to realize she was completely turned around.

Amber stopped to get her bearings, trying to take everything in, but the noise around her swallowed her thoughts. Her clumsiness got the better of her, and she bumped into a guy, sending his books and a cup of matcha tea flying to the ground.

Panicked, she said sorry and turned beetroot red, but didn't know what to do next.

The guy didn't say anything at first because he was too busy collecting his soaked books.

Amber knelt to help him but lost her balance, putting her hand on his.

They looked at each other and it felt as if they were stuck in time. They both began to blush. Amber gave him a smile, happy that he was embarrassed too.

He chuckled and said, "It's alright; these things happen."

Amber felt awful spilling his tea and told him that she owed him one.

He looked up and caught Amber's eyes. She felt an instant connection and moved forward with renewed confidence, shaking his hand with a brighter smile.

"Amber Phil," she said.

He, pausing for a moment, smiled and introduced himself as James McGill. He found the awkwardness between them faded as they exchanged a firm handshake.

As Amber gathered the rest of his books, she noticed the stack threatening to topple.

"Need help with those?" she asked.

After a brief hesitation, he handed her a few, warning that they were heavier than they looked.

She took them easily, flashing a bright smile. The stiffness between them softened as they walked together, the awkwardness giving way to an easy rhythm.

James told her the books were for business studies. He wanted to run his own company one day.

Amber lit up and told him she was studying medicine, weighing up different areas of specialty, and was considering family medicine.

James suggested that as potential doctor and businessman, they were a match made in heaven.

Amber couldn't resist smiling at him.

When they reached the classroom, Amber handed his books back to him. They exchanged friendly smiles again, and James, in the doorway, turned to her and said, "Thanks for your help, Amber. Maybe I'll see you around."

"I hope so," she replied, watching him disappear inside.

CHAPTER 2
WHERE OUR STORIES MEET

As Amber settled into university life, she kept running into James, at the library, in the corridors, in the cafe. It began to feel less like a coincidence and more like an inevitability.

One Monday in early September, Amber sat in the library, wearing a brown trenchcoat and knee high boots that caught everyone's attention. She was surrounded by piles of books, and her anatomy textbook gaped open in front of her. It was just about the time that the sunset would send the most beautiful golden light and leaves through the window.

James, being the romantic that he was, couldn't help but notice her. He walked inside.

He hesitated, not wanting to disturb her studying, but felt that he should know her.

He cleared his throat, softly saying, "Amber?"

There was no response. He tried again, louder, and in a friendlier tone. "Hi, Amber."

She looked up, met his gaze, and gave him a half-smile and a wave. He crossed over and sat beside her.

"Mind if I join you?"

She closed her book with a sigh. "Please! I was just about to leave for class, and have been struggling to get to grips with human anatomy; it's a lot to get through."

James was more laid back with his classes and thought they were simpler. Then he teased her about her classes.

They had a pleasant conversation, and Amber enjoyed the distraction. She started to tease him about his classes, saying they were more complicated than mitochondria, but James shook his head, smiling, and said, "At least, no one is counting on me to save lives."

He then noticed that Amber seemed knackered. She checked her watch, looking worried, and got up.

"I should go. Nice seeing you, James," she said, as she disappeared from view.

Coming back to the library after the winter exams, the campus buzzed with restless energy. Amber felt drained and uncertain. With her scholarship on the line and thoughts of potential failure haunting her night and day, Amber finished her first exam. She had given herself the best possible chance of passing, but hours replaying the exam in her mind had gotten to her, sending her to a place she usually went to calm herself.

SELECTING THE WRONG LOVE

Motivational phrases didn't cut it anymore. "You'll *be fine*; you always are," couldn't sit well with her anymore. She barely noticed James calling her name.

When he jogged up, concern written across his face, she finally looked up. "Amber, I haven't seen you in ages."

She shrugged weakly. His smile faded. "Are you okay?"

"I just finished an exam," she said. "It was brutal."

He gestured to a nearby bench. "I'm not a doctor, but I can listen."

They sat together. His calm presence steadied her breathing. He reminded her that the first exam is always the hardest, that she would get through it. He offered to listen, but she shook her head. He didn't push.

They sat in silence until he said softly, "Even if things don't go perfectly, it's not the end of the world. You're stronger than you think."

Her heart raced. "I can't fail," she snapped. "You don't understand."

CHAPTER 3
THE QUIET CURRENT

When Amber's anxiety flared, James didn't always recognize it. Once, trying to help, he said a bad grade wasn't the end of the world; even successful people fail. Her smile faded. She explained that there was no financial safety net back home. She couldn't afford to mess anything up. The air between them became heavy.

He gave her room to talk more about her background.

Amber took a deep breath and shared with James that she had promised her mom that she would make something of herself. Amber's mom had invested everything she had in her, and it was time for Amber to pay that back with her life; she couldn't let her mom down. Tears streamed down her face, making her voice wobbly.

When James asked about her dad, Amber lowered her

gaze; she didn't want to dwell on that part of her life. Her mom never remarried and poured all of herself into raising Amber. Hence, Amber felt like she had to succeed as an obligation to her mother.

James apologized for not knowing; he tried to help. Amber was warmed by his kindness; she told him that it wasn't his fault. James wrapped his arm around her shoulders, offering her a brief, friendly hug. Afterward, he softly brushed a strand of hair from her face. Embarrassed but earnest, he assured her that he meant what he said. Then he shared his own story: his father had left him and his mom when he was a child and never came back..

James and Amber found themselves in a moment of weightless understanding. Amber seized his hand and told him that she thought they were both carrying around a lot more emotional baggage than they showed and apologized for it. This set a pattern for a loving relationship. But none of them knew what the future held.

Amber had found belonging at the university—in James, her anchor and best friend, and someone she could have romantic feelings for. She was completely hooked on his calm self-assurance and the warmth in his eyes.

One day, seeing James leaving a study room, Amber went to meet him in the empty corridors, practically bouncing. "Hey, James."

He turned, surprised. He smiled and walked towards her with his eyes locked on hers.

Amber was overjoyed; she couldn't help but feel a deep

sense of dependence on him. She was now starting to admit to herself how much she had grown to care about him. She started talking to him about her volunteering day, and he assured her that she'd do great in her role. This made her feel less anxious.

Taking a deep breath and looking into his eyes, she asked him the question that had been brewing in her mind. "So, will you come with me?"

James asked, "Where?"

Amber's face flushed a little. She didn't want to spell out what she wanted, but said, "The clinic."

James asked if they'd go right away. Amber made it clear that they wouldn't be working; they'd be tagging along for the ride so he could see what she did. The clinic was basically the go-to place for medical students.

Before they left, Amber called ahead, letting them know she'd be bringing a friend and confirming his student badge. And just like that, their quiet current carried them forward together.

CHAPTER 4
SHADOWS OF TOMORROW

A knot of anxiety tightened in Amber's chest as she stepped out of her apartment at 7 p.m., suddenly aware that she was running late for the clinic.

James squeezed her hand playfully, offered to drive, and pulled her into a brief but reassuring hug. The simple gesture helped put things into perspective.

When they reached the car, James opened the door for her. It was a thoughtful gesture, one that lit up his face, and Amber couldn't help smiling softly.

She murmured a "Thank you" as she slid into the seat. He leaned in closer than necessary, their eyes locking for a moment; she felt the warmth of his affection.

"Don't worry about being late; there's no need to stress anymore," he said and followed up with, "You look absolutely stunning tonight."

When they got to the clinic, James stepped out first, held the door open for Amber to step onto the pavement, and ran inside after he saw she had found her footing.

Inside, two young nurses rushed over to greet Amber, who couldn't help but smile.

"Amber!" one of them called, pulling her into a warm embrace. Amber gave a strained, "Exams! I barely had time to breathe." It wasn't far from the truth.

Alice, the senior nurse, soon noticed James lingering nearby, giving Amber space. With a cheeky grin, she caught his eye and asked, "And who's this young man you've brought with you?"

Amber slipped into her white coat as Alice led them into the ward. James stayed close as Amber moved from patient to patient, taking vitals and speaking gently with each one. It was immediately clear that people felt completely at home with her. She had a gift for listening that added warmth and reassurance to the whole place, making people feel relaxed.

When she finished her rounds, Amber looked flustered. She didn't know how to respond when James said, "Honestly, you're really gifted at this. You absolutely knocked it out of the park."

Amber then explained to James that she still had at least eight years of training to go, including graduating from college, and then doing her residency.

James listened to her with wide eyes. "Eight years! That's a tremendous commitment." Lowering his voice, he added, "By the way, I have a surprise for you. But it'll have to wait."

SELECTING THE WRONG LOVE

Her face lit up with curiosity. She knew she could count on him, and whatever he had planned, she was sure she'd love it.

With her usual sass, she teased, "Don't leave me hanging."

"All in good time," he replied with a mysterious smile.

He put an arm around her shoulders, and they walked together. Amber felt a subtle shift between them—a new dynamic beginning, though neither of them quite understood it yet.

Later, when James finished his presentation in class, the professor's amazement was unmistakable, followed by thunderous applause. Amber clapped until her hands hurt, and coming down the aisle to hug him, she couldn't help but pour out a heartfelt speech.

"That was an exceptional presentation. You're a natural speaker, James, and completely mesmerized everyone."

James beamed with pride at the look of satisfaction in her eyes. "Did you really enjoy it?" he asked.

Amber's response was to wave toward the crowd of clapping people, which suggested that James was great. She didn't say anything. Amber put James back into the euphoric state he had been in during his presentation, and he found himself moving closer to her.

He leaned forward to kiss her for the very first time.

Amber froze, taken aback; she put her hand on his chest, gently pushing him away.

James didn't know what to read in her expression, so he

looked into her eyes, and was met with soft words: "I'm so proud of you, and I'm so glad you're my friend."

He tightened his hold on her, hoping to get more, but Amber didn't encourage it. He realized then that there was something deeper between them, undefined and quietly unresolved.

CHAPTER 5
HEARTS ON HOLD

By the end of their first year of college, Amber and James remained optimistic that their friendship would continue to be the anchor that gets them through anything. He found it difficult to shake off his deepening attraction to her.

One quiet Thursday night, he finally decided to take the plunge and share his feelings with the girl who sat on her favorite bench by the campus pond. The exam stress had clearly gotten to her, because she wasn't even aware of him approaching. James playfully covered her eyes from behind, just like he used to with childhood friends. "Guess who?" he said, but his voice betrayed him.

"James, don't be silly. I know it's you," Amber said in her carefree laughter. His eyes brimmed with emotion and his face strained as he sat behind her. He went pinkish red when he made a half-hearted attempt at a smile and said something else to change the subject. "Is the book any good?"

Amber turned a few pages and nodded. "It's all right."

She sensed he was holding something back and gave him space, watching him shift uncomfortably.

After a moment, she asked, "You okay?"

He nodded, swallowing hard. His thoughts were racing through his head. He couldn't look her straight in the eye, but he couldn't back down. Slowly, he edged closer to her, gathering his courage.

"Amber, I'm not sure how to say this," he said, embarrassed.

The last few months had been absolutely better than he ever thought they would be, and he couldn't pretend anymore… neither to himself nor to her. He knew it was a risk to tell her his feelings, but staying silent was even worse. The weight of their friendship and what could be at stake became painful for both of them when Amber turned to James, her heart racing with emotions she dared not express.

"James…" she started, but her voice faded. What hurt most was the longing in his eyes and the unspoken need between them.

With quiet honesty, Amber told him how extraordinary he was and how much their friendship meant to her. She couldn't bear the thought of losing it. James had imagined a different outcome… maybe even a kiss, and the disappointment of the moment sank in.

He understood that they both felt strongly for each other, but something unspoken kept them apart.

"Please, don't be troubled. I don't want to ruin what we have," Amber said for the second time, revealing the discomfort that was beginning to etch itself on her face, aware that she was hurting him. She attempted to throw her arms around James, but he moved away from her, and her arms fell limply by her sides.

James took a deep breath and stood. "It's alright. I really do understand. Some things aren't meant to be, no matter how much we wish they were."

At least he had spoken. At least there would be no *what ifs*.

That summer, Amber stayed on campus and threw herself into clinic work. By the time sophomore year began, she was more determined than ever. Her friendship with James went back to the way it was, but the underlying unease remained. Amber couldn't help stealing glances at James whenever she was on campus. She envisioned what it would be like to throw herself into his arms and give up all resistance. Hustling into the library that evening, James sensed that Amber was now ready for something more.

When he caught her staring, he smiled and pulled her attention away from her books. He sat close enough for her to feel his warm breath on her skin, sending shivers down her spine. Meeting his eyes and smiling at his playful grin, Amber confessed that she was fine, but a little anxious. Amber didn't know how to handle her growing attraction to James, so she downplayed it. She proceeded to explain to him how the second year of school was much more challenging than the first.

"You'll do great," James said in response, but his fingertips brushed her face as he tucked a strand of hair behind her ear and made her feel all sorts of happy. He said she was too smart to fail. Those words cut through her anxiety. Amber closed her book, realizing she needed a break, and she wanted to spend it with him.

Weeks passed quietly. Then one Monday, after a brutal obstetrics class, Amber was dying to get back to her room and rest. She was heading for the door when she bumped into a guy with a lot of presence.

CHAPTER 6
THE SPARK OF CHANGE

As Amber fumbled to vocalize an apology, a warm, unfamiliar fragrance caught her off guard. It was calming and invigorating at the same time, and it made her lift her eyes to see a beaming smile and a pair of piercing hazel eyes belonging to someone she had never seen before. The man was undeniably handsome; his perfectly shaped brows added to the effect. Flustered, she tried to slip past him, eager to escape.

"No worries," he said, answering her unspoken plea to be left alone.

As they nearly bumped into each other once again, a playful grin curved his lips. He remarked on the thoughtful points she made in class, which caught her off guard because she didn't know who he was. Realizing she had shared a few ideas admired by the older students, a blush crept up her cheeks, and she tucked her hair behind her ear to avoid any awkwardness.

She was still unsure about this man's identity, but he introduced himself as Levi Emir. With a smile, he extended his hand, forcing her to shake it and say hello. She tried not to make eye contact, burning with embarrassment. Pulling away from the interaction, Amber reminded herself she would not let her anxiety take over.

Levi continued, offering glowing feedback on her ideas and remarking that it seemed she cared deeply about what she did. He struck her as the kind of person who never slept and could run a marathon on a whim. Full of energy and confidence, Amber sensed he would make a great doctor, too. She shared her dream of becoming the best doctor she could be, and when Levi said he felt the same way, they agreed that there wasn't anything that could top their aspirations.

Levi picked up on her passion for working with children, asking her about her love for this job and where it came from. She felt relaxed now, dropping her initial defensiveness. It was obvious that he was passionate about his ambitions.

"That's wonderful," he said in response to all Amber had told him.

Coming from someone who had already made a name for himself, his words of encouragement and praise got to Amber.

She admitted she was from a small town: something she felt self-conscious about, worried it sounded cliché. Big dreams often felt unoriginal in high-pressure fields like medicine, and Amber knew that.

Levi's response was genuine and disarming. He told her that where she came from didn't matter, and that if she dared to dream boldly, the world would meet her halfway. His infectious optimism eased something tight inside her.

Curious now, Amber asked about him. Levi told her he was local, but the city felt too small. She teased him about being adventurous, and he played along, saying he could never be tied down, and that his heart stayed free.

They parted with casual goodbyes, promising they would probably run into each other again. Amber returned to her dorm, and Levi to the library. But something had shifted. Over the next few weeks, they kept crossing paths, and each time, Levi's confidence and enthusiasm kicked her off. She couldn't get enough of him, yet her heart remained conflicted, and James was still her friend. When James caught up with Amber, he saw her with Levi and felt a twinge of pain.

One Tuesday evening, James, mustering up the courage, approached her and brought up the topic of Levi. "So, how's Levi doing? You two seem to get along well." James tried to put on a fake smile, but Amber sensed the strain beneath it.

"He's great, smart, and we have lots of common ground," she admitted, not wanting to hurt James, but unwilling to lie.

James said very little, not wanting to seem clingy, and gave Amber space to talk more about Levi. Amber, still basking in the thrill of the conversation, got more animated when she started telling him about Levi's goal of being an obstetrician, how much they both love children, and how talking to him inspired her.

Amber's sparkling eyes gave away the truth that she was drawn to Levi, and the pain in James's eyes was no secret either. He managed a strained smile and said, "He seems like a good guy." He told her he was glad she was meeting new people. Polite as ever, he hid his hurt, and Amber realized, with a quiet ache, that her heart was changing.

CHAPTER 7
A CHOICE BETWEEN HEARTS

As the second semester drew to a close, Amber found herself caught between a growing romance with Levi and a lingering pull toward James, her best friend and the boy she once believed was her future.

Time with Levi felt exhilarating. His bold outlook challenged and elevated her, opening doors she had never considered. At the same time, Amber wrestled with the comfort of her past and the thrill and anxiety of uncertainty that new love and loyalties could cause.

One sunny Wednesday afternoon, Amber and Levi decided to relax at the campus café, and their plan of studying turned into laughter and good conversation. The window-side view filled the area and warmed the atmosphere, and they had the opportunity to discuss plans for the future. Levi brought up the possibility of Amber getting a job in New York, but she wasn't sure if she could make it in such a competitive field. Levi was undeterred and told her that she could do anything she set her mind to. Though she tried to brush it off, his confidence began to sink in.

Just then, James arrived at the café. Through the glass, he saw Amber and Levi together, laughing, close, and the sight was harder than he expected. When James approached, Levi introduced himself with a friendliness that carried a hint of rivalry. James, picking up on the vibe, nodded stiffly and looked at Amber for a sign of reassurance, but she avoided his eyes, letting him know that she had made up her mind.

"Nice to meet you," James said, faking a smile and turning back to Levi, who shook his hand with a firm, almost competitive grip.

"The pleasure's all mine," Levi said, grinning. "Amber's got a delicious taste in people."

Levi turned his attention back to Amber, sending her into a blush again. James tried to brush off his feelings of jealousy and frustration, but they got the better of him. They made him sound even more uncertain about his future when Levi asked what James was studying. James pulled out his phone, faking a call to make a hasty exit. Forcing a smile, he said that he'd catch up with them later. He didn't look back, but inside, he was completely devastated. It was like all his dreams of a future with Amber had gone up in smoke; he couldn't help but feel strongly for her.

Amber, watching James leave, was overcome with regret and sorrow. She knew she'd hurt him but saw no other way to get out of the situation she was in: being stuck between what had been and what might be.

Levi nudged her gently. "He looks like he has feelings for you."

"Levi, please," she snapped. "You don't know him."

He raised his hands. "Alright. Not my business." He studied her reaction closely, intent on keeping her attention.

That evening, unable to shake thoughts of James, Amber found him sitting alone on a bench, staring at his phone. Coming to terms with the fact that she would likely get hurt, she still went to sit beside him and tried to talk to him.

Even though she'd rehearsed what she wanted to say many times, she couldn't get anything quite right, but knew that she couldn't avoid this conversation. So, she started with a quiet "Hi."

James turned to her, giving no hint of a smile or tears. His expression was neutral; his face blank.

"Hey," he grunted, his voice lifeless; he didn't take his eyes off his phone again.

Amber sat beside him and asked, "How are you?" But James didn't move; he turned his head away. Amber gave him a light nudge and asked if he was okay, because he didn't seem to be himself.

CHAPTER 8
SHATTERED BONDS

Knowing that what she was about to say would be painful, Amber took a deep breath and turned to James.

"James, there's something I need to tell you, and I owe you honesty. This is going to be hard to hear, and I won't sugarcoat it. I care about you very much. I'm the one who hurt you, and that kills me. Because I value you so much as a friend, I won't lie to you. I want to take a chance with Levi."

James finally met her gaze, his eyes filled with sorrow and resignation. He tried to put on a brave face, but it barely held. The world had flipped upside down for him, and yet he forced himself to accept what she was saying. Amber's attempt at a gentle smile only made it worse, driving the pain deeper.

"Friends… yeah," James said quietly, his voice trembling. His smile faltered, tears threatening to spill. Unable to endure the moment any longer, he stood abruptly and walked away, leaving Amber alone on the bench.

Back in his dorm, James searched for a bottle of whiskey, hoping the numbness would dull the pain. Instead, it only deepened it. Tears streamed down his face. He slowly slid to the floor, bottle in hand, completely heartbroken. James' realization that love could be very unpredictable and unkind was painful. Some people were lucky enough to find happiness, but he was not.

James eventually passed out on the floor, the dullness of the alcohol calming him down a bit. Sleep didn't bring any peace, and his dreams were fitful and fragmented, and he couldn't remember them. By morning, his head was pounding, and it felt like his arteries were about to burst.

A week later, Levi walked Amber back to her dorm and noticed how distant she seemed. Avoiding the world wasn't his style, but he sensed something weighing on her. At her door, he asked if she was okay. She responded with a long, uncertain sigh. Amber hadn't seen James in days and had heard he hadn't shown up to class. She had tried calling him, but he never answered. The thought that something was seriously wrong terrified her.

Silence settled between them. Levi realized this wasn't the moment to push.

"Does this mean what I think it does?" he asked quietly.

Amber nodded, her voice barely a whisper, confirming she had chosen him. Taking the moment, Levi asked the question he had been holding back since the beginning.

"Amber, would you give me the honor of being my girlfriend?" and Amber, without hesitation, said, "Yes."

It was a moment she'd long imagined, but deep down, she still had James' name in her heart.

Levi beamed with happiness that Amber had chosen him, but Amber was troubled. She hadn't expected James to take the news of her going out with Levi this badly, and now, she was beginning to worry.

Levi gently wrapped his arms around her and kissed her forehead. "He'll need time; heartbreak doesn't heal overnight," he advised her.

JAMES' FEELINGS FOR AMBER HADN'T FADED, AND THREE weeks later, they nearly destroyed him. One night, James' roommate, Mike, came home to find him sprawled on the floor, surrounded by empty bottles and a suffocating heaviness. Mike knelt beside him and shook his shoulder.

"James, wake up. Are you okay?"

His face was pale, his eyes barely open. Mike noticed a piece of paper on the floor with one word scrawled across it: *AMBER*.

Refusing to let things get worse, Mike pulled James upright and spoke to him to keep him conscious.

"Come on, man. Don't let this consume you. She's not worth your life," Mike told him. James, however, couldn't handle hearing that and started to fall apart.

"Leave me alone!" he wailed, and then shouted out to the empty apartment, "She broke my heart!"

Mike dragged him to the couch and slapped his cheeks to wake him up.

"Hey, don't let a girl ruin you. Life is already tough enough." James shook his head and buried his face in a pillow.

"I love her, Mike. I love her so much, and she broke me. I can't breathe without her; nothing else matters."

Mike took a step back, unable to do anything to ease his friend's suffering. "James, I know you love her, but sometimes, love means giving up. You can't force someone to love you back."

"Why can't she love me?" James cried. "I know she does."

Mike had no answer.

CHAPTER 9

BROKEN AND UNRAVELING

James' routine of isolation, skipping classes, and drinking quickly consumed him. The emptiness of his apartment and the whiskey bottle became his only comforts after Amber's heart went to someone else. Mike couldn't watch it anymore. He called James' mother, Everett.

When Everett arrived at James' place, she was met by the overwhelming stench of stale air and broken bottles. The room was a disaster, and her son was slumped on the couch, barely coherent, staring blankly ahead, eyes glazed over. When she called out to him, he didn't stir much, half-knocked out from a whole bottle of booze.

When Everett surveyed the state of the apartment in disbelief, she asked what was wrong with him. James turned away. He was dirty, wearing stained shorts, filthy socks, and a messy shirt. Everett told him to sort himself out; he needed a shower because he smelled terrible. James didn't budge. He didn't care.

Fed up, Everett tried shaking him out of his funk. She yelled,

"You can't be serious. I didn't bring you up to behave like that. Get up and clean yourself up."

"I don't care," James growled.

Everett slapped his face, which made him sit up and stare back at her, really angry.

"What do you want from me?" he yelled.

Everett didn't back down. She told him to stop throwing his life away over someone who doesn't care about him.

James thought no one could understand the depth of his pain. He believed love had driven him mad.

"Just go; leave me alone," he said and started moving towards the bathroom. Everett got a sandwich from the campus cafeteria, realizing she hadn't eaten all day. But she wasn't done. She needed answers.

Spotting Amber sitting alone in the cafeteria stopped her cold. She recognized her instantly from James' photos.

"You're Amber, right?" Everett asked, her voice icy.

"Yes?" Amber replied, startled.

"I'm James' mother," Everett said. "And whatever you've done to my son, you won't get away with it."

Amber stared, speechless.

As Everett turned to leave, Amber called out. "Wait. Is that a threat?"

Everett walked back to Amber, her face inches away from Amber's. "Take it however you want; no one hurts my son. Especially not someone like you."

Amber started getting hot-headed and said something that made Everett raise one of her eyebrows. "What do you mean, someone like me? This isn't my business."

"Please, don't blame me, I—" Amber continued to speak, but Everett cut her off.

"Enough! Stay away from my son. You've done enough," she yelled.

She stormed out, leaving Amber shaken and alone.

That night, Amber fought the urge to call James. She knew his mother was likely still with him, and the last thing he needed was more chaos.

When Everett returned to the dorm, James sat silently on the couch. She began to clean the bottles.

"How can you live like this? Is any girl really worth destroying yourself over?" she asked.

James didn't respond; he just muttered words to himself. Everett asked him to repeat what he had said, and James told her that she wouldn't get it. Everett cut loose with something close to anger.

"You think I don't know about heartbreak? You think you're the only one who's ever been through a rough time? You're not smarter than me, James. I raised you."

James couldn't deny that, but it didn't make his pain any better. James wanted to be left alone and buried his face in the couch.

Everett was firm. "I would if I could, but I can't. You need to sort yourself out before you do serious harm to yourself. The brutal truth is that Amber doesn't love you, and I'm the only one who cares. But you need to face it."

Her words settled in. Everett stayed for the next three weeks, slowly helping him recover. He was still fragile, and she caught him sneaking drinks, but he was beginning to heal.

CHAPTER 10
AWAKENING DESIRE

James had been quietly piecing himself back together while Amber's relationship with Levi was in full bloom. After the turmoil of the past, Amber found herself falling for Levi in ways she hadn't expected.

One Friday evening, they planned a study session in Amber's dorm. Coming into the date with a clear idea of wanting to take the next step, Amber heard a soft knock at her door and, opening it, was greeted by Levi's beaming smile and the breathtaking sight of a mammoth bouquet of roses that all but hid him from view, making her catch her breath.

Amber's heart was overjoyed. She exclaimed, "Are these for me?" as she took in the extravagant roses. Levi, handing her the bouquet, made a comment so charming that it made her eyes sparkle.

"They're beautiful. Thank you," she said, and her cheeks turned a shade of pink with happiness.

For a fleeting second, thoughts of someone else who had been left behind started to get stuck in her mind, but Amber brushed them away and accepted the flowers and the compliment with a grateful smile. She leaned over the flowers, took his face in her hands for a gentle kiss, savoring the warmth and the promises of his touch.

"Come in," she said, stepping aside.

Levi strode into the apartment, gave the space a bit of a once-over, and couldn't help but eye the bed with a cheeky grin. Amber busily rearranged the flowers in a pitcher and didn't say much, probably distracted by the way she would soon be wrapped up in Levi's side. She came closer to him, putting her arm around his waist, leaving no doubt about what she wanted. Levi searched her face, silently asking if she was sure.

Nerves and excitement collided as Amber met his eyes. She smiled, and he mirrored it; the moment suspended between hesitation and desire.

Levi leaned in and kissed her. Amber melted into it, letting go of her worries. When he whispered that he loved her, her heart soared. At that moment, she knew they belonged to each other.

The world narrowed to quiet breaths and gentle touches as Amber surrendered to the closeness between them. That night, Amber had her very first taste of true intimacy. The incredible pleasure and closeness woke something new inside her and confirmed what her heart already knew: that Levi was the one. They spent the night wrapped in each other's arms.

The soft morning light streamed through the window as Amber lay beside Levi, watching him sleep. A deep sense of peace and belonging she'd never known before overcame her. She called him perfect.

Levi woke up, his sleepy eyes locked onto hers. He pulled her into a gentle kiss and said, "Good morning, beautiful."

Amber, overflowing with happiness, whispered back, "I love you," sealing the words with a tender kiss. As the days and weeks passed, their love grew stronger, developing into a real, lasting bond.

CHAPTER 11
WHEN LIFE CHANGES COURSE

As Amber and Levi's time at the university came to a close, they'd become the couple that everyone looked up to. James still seethed with an unfulfilled yearning for what he once had with Amber.

FOUR YEARS WENT BY BEFORE AMBER FINISHED MEDICAL school. The graduation day was a day of unrelenting pride, sunlight, and celebrations. The crowning moment of Amber's hard work was, of course, getting her bachelor's degree. Amber's mum sat in the audience with Levi, beaming and whooping with joy as Amber walked onto the stage to pick up her diploma and medal.

When Levi shouted, "That's my girl," it caught her off guard and took the breath from her. Her speech was short and flowed with sincerity, and immediately after, she dashed off the stage to throw herself into the arms of the two people who meant the world to her.

LEVI TEASED HER, SAYING HE WAS TRYING TO EMBARRASS her, but really, he just wanted everyone to know just how proud he was of her. Coming at the top of her class ensured that Amber's dream of becoming a top-notch pediatrician would be a reality. Amber gave Levi and her mum a hug, and her mum's face lit up with pride.

"You did the impossible," she said, holding Amber close and making Amber feel like a little kid again, safe in her mother's embrace.

Levi watched the bond between these two women and wasn't sure he could ever fully put it into words. Gently, he pulled Amber back into his arms, said she'd be a fantastic doctor, and was counting down the days until he could call her his again. When Amber's mother looked at her, she couldn't help noticing how much she'd changed. She had found happiness in Levi. They went out to celebrate.

SELECTING THE WRONG LOVE

Five weeks into the summer, Amber spent nearly every day volunteering at the city hospital. One Friday evening, Levi arrived to pick her up and immediately sensed something was wrong. Her face was pale, and her expression anxious.

"Are you okay?" he asked, drawing her into his arms.

She hesitated, then pulled a small object from her pocket and placed it in his hand. Levi stared at the pregnancy test, his breath catching as he saw the two lines.

"A baby?" he asked softly. "Is it really ours?"

Amber could barely meet his eyes, overwhelmed. Then Levi smiled, wide and certain. He told her he didn't care whether it was a boy or a girl. When Amber and Levi locked eyes, they both knew they were meant to be a family. She threw herself into his arms, spilling her feelings out to him, and getting completely swept away by the idea of their future together. With him by her side, she felt safe and adored.

Realizing that they had a lot to learn about each other, Amber was determined to make the next chapter in their lives a beautiful one. She wanted to make their commitment to each other official.

Two months into her pregnancy, Amber and Levi got married in a quaint, intimate, outdoor ceremony, in front of just their closest friends and family. Amber couldn't care less about the big picture; she was far more interested in nurturing her baby and the home they were building together.

James, still haunted by the past, abandoned his business ambitions and turned toward medical school, driven by something unresolved. He left for Europe and settled in Monaco, determined to prove himself. Despite the distance, thoughts of Amber lingered, a quiet ache that never fully faded.

CHAPTER 12

THE WEIGHT OF SACRIFICE

When Amber and Levi brought their newborn son, Lucas, home from the hospital seven months after their wedding, they could not have been happier. Lucas stole the spotlight immediately. He had inherited his mother's piercing blue eyes and delicate features, and his bright, bubbly nature seemed to light up every room.

Levi was completely besotted with his son. Amber and Lucas were the two most precious things in his life, and he would do anything to protect and care for them.

Perceptive as ever, Levi noticed a quiet unease beneath Amber's calm exterior. While holding Lucas one afternoon, he turned to her and asked if everything was alright. Amber hesitated. Though she was deeply devoted to her family, the dreams she once held so tightly had not disappeared.

When Levi teased her gently, she tried to brush it off, but eventually gave in. She admitted she missed the hospital and longed to care for children again. At the same time, she knew her family needed her more than ever. Wrapping her arms around Levi and Lucas, she drew strength from their closeness.

Levi reassured her immediately. When he finished his residency, he promised he would do everything he could to help her return to medicine. His sincerity caught her off guard. "You promise?" she asked, smiling softly. Levi nodded without hesitation.

A year later, and the pressure on her, juggling a half-time job in a supermarket and a full-time job in customer services, was becoming too much. Amber's mother worried that Amber's own aspirations had faded away when Levi became an obstetrician at McGill Hospital after completing his residency. She was filled with memories of the joy she felt whenever Amber came visiting, greeting her with a beaming smile.

For Amber, the discomforting pangs of envy and uncertainty about her own future began to creep in. Amber devoted her time to her family and found happiness in small moments; the contrast between their lives grew sharper as Levi worked longer hours. Amber reassured herself that what she had before was quite good, and was still grateful for the love of her family.

Levi sat down with Amber one chilly night on the porch swing, exhausted but at peace, and laid his head on her shoulder. He wished that every night could be like this, and there was no doubting that Amber derived happiness from the simple things in life. Amber started to mull over her own ambitions. Were they a thing of the past, gone into hazy memories? Levi tried to assure her that they would definitely reach their goals. But the relentless pressures of life sent them in different directions.

Years passed. Amber's pride in her son was a reality, but her marriage couldn't be said the same. As Levi's job took more of his time, Amber started to feel disheartened and taken for granted. The once warm and lively home was now freezing and empty, and Amber spent most of her evenings sitting in front of the TV. The silence of the house was painful.

Glancing at her life as a mother and all the sacrifices she made, Amber started questioning Levi's fidelity to her and their relationship. As Amber thought about her place in the life of her family, she wondered if the love she was giving them was enough. Her growing uncertainty was eating away at her, and she couldn't shake the nagging suspicion that something was wrong.

Amber decided to surprise Levi at work one day. To her dismay, she saw him with a beautiful young nurse who seemed overly familiar with him. Sadness surged through her.

She approached with a forced cheer. "Hello, babe."

Levi and the nurse were startled. Amber commented on the nurse's physical proximity to him. Levi brushed it off, explaining that the nurse was new. But Amber's irritation spilled over. When Levi tried to hug her and ask if everything was okay at home, she pulled away and left without another word.

Levi stood in the hospital lobby, unsettled and confused.

That night, he returned home late to find Amber and Lucas asleep. Unsure how to bridge the growing gap between them, he slept on the couch, the sense of distance lingering heavily.

CHAPTER 13
FRACTURES IN THE SILENCE

By the following month, the strain in their household had reached a breaking point. Years of unspoken resentment, missed conversations, and avoided glances had hollowed Amber's emotional world. The idea of a life defined by sacrifice and silence felt unbearable.

In a desperate attempt to reconnect, Levi insisted there was no one else. He told Amber his heart belonged to her, but his words came out rough, edged with exhaustion. Amber could not listen anymore. She cut him off and left the room.

Left alone with his own helplessness, Levi struggled to sleep and lost his appetite, the weight of their disconnection pressing down on him.

In the middle of the night, he wandered outside, pacing beneath the streetlights. His movements were all over the place, and he appeared to be arguing with himself.

Amber fell onto her bed, crying hysterically, and felt a deep ache of grief and yearning in her heart. Even though she still loved Levi and thought of him as her soulmate, the pain of their distance and her shattered dreams made it impossible for her to picture a way back to happiness with him.

As the weeks dragged on, Levi started working longer hours and was away from home later into the night. He couldn't stand the silence anymore. So, he tried to fill the void with work. Amber was being tormented by jealousy and loneliness. Nightmares haunted her, and she woke in tears, terrified at the thought of losing everything.

One Saturday night, overwhelmed by anxiety, Amber arranged for a sitter, and drove to the hospital after Lucas went to bed. By the time she arrived, it was nearly midnight. In the dim corridors, she followed familiar paths until she heard a woman's laughter. She froze, then forced herself forward.

She eavesdropped on the conversation between Levi and the young nurse, Emily, who both sounded like they were having a fantastic time together. The anger and heartbreak that Amber had been carrying around finally boiled over. She called out to Levi and turned a corner to see him turning around. Emily smirked, as if she had just won a game.

Levi was caught off guard and asked Amber what she was doing there, but Amber asked him to tell Emily to leave. Emily didn't budge. Amber lost her temper and told Levi that she needed to talk to him, her voice trembling.

Levi, embarrassed and trying to calm her down, said he was having a rough night, and they could talk at home, but

Amber wouldn't be put off. Emily interjected, her tone unmistakable. Amber blocked her out and focused on Levi, grabbing his arm, her hands shaking all over.

"Please," she said, her voice breaking with a yearning for reconnection. For a moment, Levi hesitated, then he started to follow her to a quieter part of the office, his expression distant.

Amber questioned Levi's loyalty, asking him if there was someone else in his life. Amber's accusations shocked Levi. He couldn't understand how she could believe he would betray her. He cupped her face, asking her to look at him, but when she pulled away, defeated, his frustration broke through. He asked if everything he had done for her and their son wasn't enough proof of his loyalty.

Levi felt like he had been running on a treadmill, exhausting himself to make life better for those he loved, but he didn't get enough back. He cut Amber off when she tried to talk to him; he didn't want a lecture at that moment. The space between them was starting to feel insurmountable.

CHAPTER 14
LOVE IN THE COLD

Years of pent-up anger finally exploded, and Amber didn't flinch at Levi's rough words as she stood face-to-face with him. She told him that her life wasn't turning out the way she had envisioned. He wasn't the only one making sacrifices. When he was away, she was taking care of Lucas, the house and putting her dreams on hold, and working jobs that didn't fulfill her. Money wasn't going to make up for any of it. If he thought sending money was the same thing as loving her and their son, then he didn't understand what she was asking for.

Raw words filled the air—things she couldn't take back. Levi responded with a sharp, snarky laugh and suggested they go their separate ways. Amber couldn't comprehend splitting up, especially with a child involved. It felt surreal. The firmness of Levi's expression and his glacial stare told her he meant every word.

She tried to ask what he was saying, but he turned away, nodding.

"You heard me, Amber."

The thought of divorce shook her to the core.

"You can't seriously be asking for a divorce. What about our boy? He needs his father."

"I'm not vanishing," Levi cut in. "I'll always be there for him. But this isn't working. We're killing each other slowly."

Amber tried to bring up their vows, tried to reach for something that still felt sacred, but her words were drowned when Levi's phone rang.

He glanced at the screen, muttered something about an emergency, and said, "We'll talk when I get back."

He turned away, exchanged a few words with Emily as he passed her, and disappeared down the hallway.

Amber left the hospital completely reeling. That night, she couldn't sleep, clinging to the fragile hope that this fight wouldn't be the end of their marriage.

At dawn, when the door finally opened, she asked the question burning inside her the moment Levi stepped in. "Is this about Emily? She seems very interested in you."

Levi dropped his bag, startled. He told her she scared him, and that he didn't understand why she kept bringing up Emily. Their problems weren't about Emily. They were about them.

They weren't the same anymore. The romance was gone.

He didn't know how else to say it. Amber gripped the dining table to steady herself. She told him they had to try, and that keeping their relationship alive was up to both of them. She told him to think about it.

Levi said things had changed, and he didn't know if it was stress, exhaustion, or life itself. All he ever wanted was to give them a happy life, and he still did, but Amber shot back at him, claiming that life was coming apart at the seams.

Feeling exasperated, Levi looked at her with dull and exhausted eyes. "I don't know what to do anymore," he said. "I'm too knackered to think straight. I need a nap before I collapse." He went up the stairs and told Amber that they'd talk later. Due to his hectic lifestyle and reserved personality, the arguments they were having started to dwindle, but the warmth of their relationship had disappeared. Amber was struggling to get in touch with Levi.

Amber clung to the hope that they could revive their crumbling relationship. Coming home early one night, Levi gave her a chance, and as they went to bed together, Amber seized the moment of respite and decided to speak softly to his heart. She beamed at him and whispered a kiss on his shoulder.

Levi had been lying on the bed for a moment, engrossed in a book, but putting it down, he sighed and turned to her.

"Years, lots of years, and lots we've shared together."

Amber asked him to tell her what had made him push her away. "Why throw it all away?" Amber asked. "Can't we try to fix it? I love you."

She begged him with an expression that spoke to his pain and humanity—something that he hadn't been focusing on enough.

It was hard not to notice when someone really got down to the heart of things. Coming from a place of love, Levi blurted something out of the blue that knocked Amber off balance. "I love you. I never stopped." This made her feel hopeful that they might be able to fix things.

CHAPTER 15
BEHIND CLOSED DOORS

While Amber fought to save her marriage, Emily had a very different vision of the man she wanted. Coming from a wealthy background, Emily was drawn to Levi's status and his money. She had no interest in his family or anyone else's. She wasn't the kind of woman who stepped aside for anyone.

Levi tried to avoid being alone with her at work, but their paths crossed constantly. Exhaustion clung to him, and the painkillers he had been taking made his weariness unmistakable. Seizing the moment, Emily sidled up to him with a dazzling smile and got his attention by stroking his arm.

"You look stressed," she said, softly massaging his forearm. How tightly her uniform fitted her body made him feel a bit weak in the knees. Her playfulness, smile, and low, soothing voice made him feel torn.

After his shift, unwinding with a drink in the break room was exactly what he thought he needed, and he couldn't face going back home to the strained state of his house, full of unspoken words and heavy silence.

Leaning in closer, she laid on her persuasive tone and said, "Come on, you're shattered. You deserve to relax."

Without waiting for a response, she wrapped her arm around his waist and led him into the empty break room. Levi couldn't say no when she offered him champagne. Being knackered from a long day of work, he accepted the glass she offered and downed it in one go.

Being a medical practitioner, Levi shouldn't have been drinking at all. But he imagined that one glass wouldn't hurt anyone. The combination of champagne and his painkillers made his mind go all over the place. He couldn't seem to find the right words.

Emily gave him a massage, refilled his glass, and poured him a third one when that was finished. Levi started to feel disoriented.

"We all need to escape sometimes," Emily said softly, and then asked, "Are you alright?"

He tried to answer, but his words came out muffled, and he began to struggle to stay upright. Emily helped him up, guided him out of the break room into an on-call room meant for rest, and locked the door behind them. Three glasses of bubbly and a whole lot of medication after a very long day left him reeling around the place and completely turned around.

She made him sit down on a bed; she pressed him against the wall, and said, "Let's get you somewhere to rest before anyone sees you."

The dim lighting in the room was pleasant and calming, but his flushed face, racing heart, and inability to move weren't doing much to calm him down.

"Are you okay?" Emily asked him again, with a wicked grin. She kissed his neck and ran her tongue along his collarbone. He couldn't stop wanting her, and Emily picked up on that really well.

"Let me look after you," she said, gently sliding her hands down his shirt, all the way to his waist.

"What are you doing?" Levi blurted out, but he knew exactly what she was up to.

Emily muffled his protests with a kiss, not letting him get a word out, and took over completely.

She whispered, "You'll love it," and pressed herself against him, sending him reeling with the heat and the closeness of her body. She didn't even give him a chance to hear what she said into his ear: "You're mine." She started undressing him; he didn't know how to stop her.

Levi managed to get out a desperate plea. "Please, don't."

But Emily tuned him out and shut him down with another kiss that left him gasping for air. She kept repeating that everything would be alright. She started pushing him towards the bed, then she took off her clothes and got on top of him before he could change his mind.

Emily was getting what she wanted, as her heart raced with excitement. She wanted Levi's whole heart, not just his body, and she was willing to do whatever it took to get him.

CHAPTER 16
HAUNTED BY DESIRE

Basically half-naked, Levi woke up. He was still feeling the effects of the champagne and wasn't expecting the sight of Emily lying next to him. Seeing her sent him into a panic, and he tried to squirm away, but Emily woke up and caught him.

Fragments of the previous night came flooding into Levi's mind, and he tried to piece them together. But what was real and what was just his imagination was still a mystery. Emily raised her eyebrow and let silence fill the space between them.

Levi said, "Emily, tell me what's going on." He began to get sickly pale as the realization of what might have happened began to sink in.

Emily grinned even wider, saying, "We had some fun, that's all."

This made Levi recoil from her, putting as much space between them as he could. He asked her, "What are you saying exactly?" Emily laid back and showed him her half-naked body, which made it crystal clear what had transpired between them.

Levi asked what time it was and fumbled for his phone, desperate to find a way out of the situation. As he spotted it by the lampstand, it started to ring. He looked at the screen. It was 5:15 a.m. Seeing Amber's name on the screen made guilt hit him hard.

Emily's voice dripped with mockery as she asked, "Can she really make you happy, Levi?"

He answered the call. Amber's words were soothing. She invited him to come home and join her in bed. Levi sat up straight, thinking he was going to have a pleasant day with his wife, but Emily threw herself on him and started begging him to kiss her.

She kept asking him to repeat the "amazing performance" he gave her the night before and wasn't willing to drop the idea that he had feelings for her. He resisted, but she got more provocative, enjoying the back-and-forth. Levi said to Amber on the call, "Babe, I'll call you back, something's come up!" He ended the call and pushed Emily away.

Emily teased him again, saying he had lost his mind over her and had realized how much he cared for her. Pressing herself against his hand, she made it clear what she was after. "Your wife would never let you do that," she said. Levi pulled his hand back. "Damn it!" he exclaimed.

Coming across as confident and aggressive, Emily, undeterred, pressed herself against him once again, forcing him back onto the bed, and saying things he didn't want to hear about his wife. She started to grind against him.

CHAPTER 17
THE WEIGHT OF SECRETS

Levi struggled to get his thoughts straight. The events of the previous night were still hazy, and Emily's version of what had happened did nothing to reassure him. Doubt gnawed at him as Emily appeared again, far too close for comfort.

Emily stepped nearer with a teasing tone. "Oh, then what do you want?"

The sight of her nibbling on her bottom lip sent Levi's thoughts into a whirlwind. He didn't know if he had been harboring feelings for Emily, and now, they were beginning to surface.

The partial view of her body didn't offer clarity either. He felt torn between his base desires and his moral code. Levi gathered up what was left of his composure and told her to back off.

"Whatever happened last night was a mistake, and that's all," he said. Emily opened her mouth to dispute his claim, but he was already heading for the door.

Coming home to a silent house offered no comfort, though the sound of soft music drifting from upstairs pulled him forward. He climbed the stairs with a heavy heart, unable to shake the image of Emily from his mind.

The bedroom door was slightly ajar. Inside, Amber sat at her vanity in a white nightgown, brushing her dark hair. Levi stopped in the doorway, frozen by the sight of her. Guilt washed over him so sharply it nearly brought him to tears.

Sensing something was wrong, Amber turned and searched his face. His expression revealed nothing of the truth weighing him down.

When she asked if he was alright, Levi nodded. He told her he was just tired. The lie felt poisonous.

Trying to comfort him, Amber invited him to sit, guiding him gently to the bed. She knelt behind him and began to massage his shoulders, slowly and tenderly.

When she leaned in to kiss him, he turned away.

"What's wrong?" She received no response. His jaw was clenched, his eyes were empty… He was haunted. Despair and hopelessness welled up inside him.

Levi told her he was exhausted and needed to rest, which wasn't enough to satisfy Amber's growing worry. Knowing that pressing him for answers may turn him away from her, she gave him some space.

"Go take a shower and get some sleep. I'll give you the space you need."

But the emptiness in his eyes stayed with her long after he left the room. He had never been this distant. Her thoughts drifted unwillingly to Emily... to what that woman might be capable of. Dread settled in.

CHAPTER 18
IRREVOCABLE CONSEQUENCES

Levi knew he could not avoid Emily for long. A week passed faster than he expected, each day tightening the knot in his chest. Monday morning in the break room brought reality crashing down. Emily appeared beside him, dropping something near his feet. Levi ignored it, focusing on his coffee, pretending she wasn't there.

She didn't let him escape.

"Are you really going to ignore me," she asked, "after everything we've been through?"

He set his cup down and finally met her stare, bracing himself.

Emily's satisfaction was unmistakable. She nudged the object closer. When Levi looked down, recognition hit him instantly. A pregnancy test.

"What do you want from me?" Levi asked, turning pale as

he stared back at Emily, completely caught off guard. Emily told him to look again. When he did, he couldn't miss the two pink lines.

"It's yours," Emily said with absolute certainty.

She went on to explain that when she missed her period, she thought something was seriously wrong, so she took the test, and now, she was sure that she was carrying Levi's child. Levi tried to think about the events that led to the pregnancy but was unable to string the events together. He asked Emily when she had taken the pregnancy test. She said that she had taken the test three different times.

Levi's world began to spin out of control. He was aware that Emily wouldn't agree to an abortion. In a desperate attempt to find an alternative, he asked her to calm down, but she was completely uncooperative and furious.

"It's too late for regrets," she said flatly.

The emptiness of the room closed in on him. Pale and sweating, Levi understood there was no escaping what lay ahead. Emily was counting on his sense of duty to stop him from running away.

Coming from a strained marriage and a home life he was desperately trying to mend, he now had to prepare himself for a life he never asked for, full of entanglements.

He looked at Emily and awkwardly said, "I'll take care of it." He walked away in an attempt to find some peace and quiet, but he was unsure if he'd find any.

CHAPTER 19
THE CHOICE UNVEILED

Levi could tell that something was wrong the moment Emily hurried into his office. It was not her usual style. She was clutching an envelope, and Levi, perceptive as ever, knew this wouldn't be new information. Still, Emily toyed with him, waving the envelope around just long enough to hook his attention.

She pulled out an ultrasound image, unfolding it with a flourish. Her face lit up as she looked at it.

"Since you already have one son," she said brightly, "the universe is sending you a daughter."

Emily was brimming with energy, desperate for him to share her excitement.

Levi felt unsteady. His life had been turned upside down, yet when he looked at the image, a spark of emotion ran through him. "A daughter," he murmured, pride slipping into his voice before he could stop it. Coming from a place of faith, he believed every child was a gift. Still, he wasn't ready to make promises or commit to anything, least of all, to someone who seemed to expect him to sign away his life without hesitation.

Emily started talking about names, asking what he thought they should call their baby. She suggested "Angela" or "Irene", saying Angela sounded angelic, and Irene sounded elegant. As she talked, she watched him closely. She caught the hesitation in his eyes.

She tried to sound casual, but she wasn't going to let Levi wriggle himself out of the situation. She was counting on a direct response, tapping her foot impatiently, but Levi was stuck between his son, his unborn daughter, and the two women who had basically taken over his life.

Emily, sensing his confusion, tried to step in. "Tell your wife you're expecting a girl, and that you're planning to leave her, to be with me."

Levi knew that Amber was a mild person who couldn't compete with Emily's fiery personality.

"I'm not sure," Levi said hesitantly. He was not sure how to navigate the situation.

Emily took his hands and gently pressed them on her stomach. She told him that his unborn daughter wouldn't wait for him to sort anything out; she'd barge her way into the picture. She gave Levi a smile and then used guilt and promises of a happy future to soften him up.

SELECTING THE WRONG LOVE

The following weeks were a nightmare for Levi. Emily refused to give him space, throwing herself at him at every opportunity, reminding him of what she believed he owed her.

CHAPTER 20
ECHOES OF BETRAYAL

Levi's home was heavy with silence. Amber's fork clinking against her plate was the only sound cutting through the silence as Levi sat at the table with her and their son. When Amber looked up to meet his gaze, Levi noticed her red-rimmed eyes and the depth of pain he couldn't escape.

Usually so composed, Amber was now on the brink of breaking. She set down her cutlery and looked at him squarely.

"You need to decide, Levi. Don't tell me you're still uncertain. You have a wife and a son, don't you?"

He knew she deserved the truth, even if it destroyed her. Conflicting emotions churned inside him, but the choice had already been made.

"Soon," he said quietly, "I'll be a father to a daughter."

Amber hadn't suspected anything, so she wasn't prepared for the bombshell.

"A daughter?" she asked in almost a whisper. The news of Levi's betrayal and the child he'd fathered with another woman left her completely speechless and deathly pale. Pressing her lips tight and fighting back the tears, Amber said nothing.

Levi went on speaking. "It happened; I won't deny it anymore. Amber, I'm sorry, but we're going to need a divorce. I've made up my mind to go forward with Emily, and I must take responsibility for my actions."

She thought about all the sacrifices she had made for him. She pointed out that she had given him everything, and was disappointed at how he chose to repay her.

Her control snapped. She slapped him... then again. Levi grabbed her wrist, pulling her into his arms. She fought to release herself from his hold, and in her rage, she bit his chest.

"You selfish bastard!" she yelled and told him that he didn't care about destroying their lives, as long as he was happy.

She asked him to let her go, but he wouldn't. Coming to terms with the situation, Amber collapsed into his arms, defeated and exhausted. She pondered how Emily had managed to win him over.

LEVI HAD MADE HIS CHOICE, AND THERE WAS NOTHING Amber could do to change it. He'd have to go live with Emily.

He, however, promised to be there for Amber and their son. This promise meant nothing to Amber. She didn't want any sympathy or handouts from him. If he couldn't give her his full love and commitment, then it would be better for him to be with Emily. She convinced herself to believe that he'd never find anyone else like her.

CHAPTER 21
WHEN LOVE ISN'T ENOUGH

Levi reached for Amber, his hands instinctively trying to close the space that existed between them. The urge to cling to her and never let her go surged wildly inside him. He didn't want to let go; he didn't want to lose her. Amber jerked away, her eyes blazing.

"Don't touch me," she yelled.

Levi froze. His breathing turned uneven, and when he tried to speak, his voice cracked.

He laid his heart bare, insisting she was his only love, and that his heart never stopped beating for her. He admitted that he had chosen a selfish path that would haunt him for the rest of his life. Amber clamped her jaw shut, her hands trembling at her sides.

He tried to justify what happened with Emily, then realized how trapped he was in a prison of empty promises and obligations he didn't understand. The love he had for Emily wasn't honest, and he had broken the one person who didn't deserve to be hurt—Amber. Levi started to cry, begging for forgiveness. His hands hovered inches from hers; he didn't want to get any closer.

For the first time, Levi understood that apologies would never be enough. Amber's reaction was immediate and brutal. Someone who once loved him deeply now wanted to scream, curse him, and erase him from her life entirely.

Beneath the anger, there was something else—a raw, aching reminder of the love they had. It made her quiver as she talked. She asked him what it was like to be second best to the man who once told her she was everything. His countenance answered for him. Amber moved closer, locking eyes with him. For a moment, Levi thought she would collapse into his arms. Instead, she shoved him away.

"You've caused me so much pain, Levi," she said. "I gave you happiness and a lovely son. And everything else had been a loss."

She told him that designer clothes and money would never fill the emptiness he had created.

"People who destroy their partners aren't given a second chance, and I won't be your second choice when regret starts gnawing away at you."

Amber turned and walked away from him. Every step felt more painful because she was physically and emotionally pulling herself away from him.

Levi, who was used to being the one in charge, was now

unable to say anything to stop her. If he did, it would be the end of them both. He started to feel the sense of losing someone for the very first time in his life.

When Amber found out that Levi wasn't going to fight for her, she came to terms with the fact that he didn't love her anymore, and it hurt more.

Levi remained frozen, crushed by the emptiness that Amber's absence would create. The world seemed to be punishing him for letting her slip away. He pressed his hand against his chest where hers had just been, and he was slapped with the stark reality that there wasn't warmth there anymore. He went over all the memories of Amber and their time together. None of them were pleasant anymore, since they were now just reminders of the promises he made and didn't keep.

Thinking about Emily was now a persistent reminder that he had made a choice, and that he had given up on the thing he loved to tie himself to someone he didn't even know. He had a basic idea of her but didn't know her fears, dreams, or favorite color. Yet, he had decided that obligation was more critical. He had destroyed the one thing that truly mattered to him.

As the weight of his choices crashed down on him, he wondered whether loyalty without love was worth the cost. In anguish, he hurled his phone aside and slammed his fist into the wall.

CHAPTER 22
WHEN LOVE RUNS OUT

Six months later, Amber and Levi barely resembled the passionate lovers they once were. When they appeared in court, the intimacy was gone. All that remained was distance and emotional detachment.

The courtroom was tense and unyielding. When the judge asked if either of them had anything to say, Amber's response was sharp and final. She wanted the papers signed. She signed them with force, the pen dragging across the page as if carving words into stone.

Levi leaving her for a nurse was something Amber had been forced to accept, but her anger had turned inward. She now despised herself for the depths she sank to for someone who didn't care for her, and who had now been revealed as a homewrecker.

As she handed him the signed documents, Amber looked

him right in the eye, spewing venomous hatred at him and his girlfriend. Levi was wracked with guilt; he hesitated as he signed the papers. For a moment, he almost changed his mind, but looking at Amber made him feel tired and sad, and he said to her, "You and my son will always matter to me." However, Amber was not going to be swayed by empty words. She scorned him. The silence as the divorce was finalized was suffocating. There was no sense of closure for either of them.

Levi moved into a luxury apartment in the heart of the city, ensuring Emily, heavily pregnant with their daughter, Amelia, had everything she needed. Emily was nearing her due date. She was proud of her pregnancy but was completely exhausted by the aches and pains. Levi did his absolute best to support her. She and Levi had been doing a great job of keeping their rekindled romance under wraps. They really wanted to have a safe delivery of their baby.

When Emily was 39 weeks and four days pregnant, she came home from a long day and started to feel unwell. She began pacing back and forth in her living room and rubbing her back. Her discomfort alarmed Levi. He watched her closely, concerned, as he tried to be supportive.

Emily didn't take his attempts to placate her very well. However, he tried to ensure that she was okay; he also had to shake off thoughts of Amber. He suggested that she try lying down for a bit.

Just then, Emily's water suddenly broke, and she couldn't help but panic. "Oh my God, Levi! My water just broke."

She looked down and saw far more blood than expected.

Panic tore through her, shock rippled through her body, and fear overtook her completely. After a frantic outburst of curses, her strength faltered. Her lips trembled.

"Levi, I'm scared."

Knowing they must get to the hospital immediately, Levi took her hand and guided her toward the elevator. "You're going to be okay, I promise," he said, trying to calm her down, but Emily was falling apart at the seams. She had never been pregnant before, and desperately wanted this baby, mainly because it was Levi's, and the thought of losing him filled her with horror. She clung to him and begged him not to leave her. Levi thought it was just fear and pain, but Emily was dead serious.

CHAPTER 23
HEARTS IN TRANSITION

The thought of losing Levi had once been unbearable for Emily. She couldn't imagine dismantling the life they'd built together. Now, as she was hurtling through the city in the back of the car, she could feel her baby moving down her pelvis—a sign that labor was just around the corner. Being a medical practitioner, she thought she was ready, but as a first-time mom, her nerves were really getting the better of her. She kept praying for her baby's safety. Every jarring turn and pothole made her squirm in agony.

Breathing exercises didn't seem to calm her racing thoughts anymore, and Levi's erratic driving sent her completely off balance. In the rearview mirror, he checked up on Emily, his face a picture of worry.

He said to her, "Just hang in there; we're almost at the hospital. Dr. Rex is waiting for us."

Since he was the baby's father, a colleague of his was going to be responsible for the birth.

Between the groans of pain, Emily's grip on the armrests got tighter, and she said, "She'd better be here soon, Levi."

She got visibly more distressed as the pain surged through her. She wiped the sweat from her forehead and the back of her neck, but forced herself to breathe through the pain.

"Make sure they have a bed ready for me."

"I will," Levi promised, tightening his hold on the steering wheel as he pulled into the hospital entrance and headed for the emergency room.

Inside, Levi flagged down a nurse and a team of orderlies, who swiftly brought in a wheelchair, and Emily was whisked away to the delivery room, where Levi went with her, holding her hand.

Emily was reassured by both Levi and Dr. Rex that the pain would be gone soon since it was a natural birth. Emily's doctor and the soft touch of Levi on her forehead gave her the strength to push her daughter into the world. Hearing that the little one was perfectly healthy was the most heartwarming news.

Seeing her newborn daughter, Amelia, Emily was overwhelmed with joy. "She's perfect," she declared.

Levi, who had not felt the same immediate bond with his son at birth, found himself overwhelmed by the fragility of his daughter. Watching her tiny chest rise and fall, he felt a renewed sense of purpose. He would protect her. He would provide for her.

Though the pain of his divorce from his ex-wife still lingered, Levi told himself that they'd be fine. The brand-new memory of baby Amelia in his heart had eased much of his nervousness.

Emily lovingly called Amelia "our little girl" and tenderly stroked her cheek, saying something that filled Levi's heart with happiness. He thought Amelia was as beautiful as she was and had Levi's eyes.

In the months following the separation, Amber found herself drowning in unpaid bills and endless chores. The emptiness of the house was exhausting in a way she never anticipated. Coming to terms with losing the home, car, and financial stability she once had was something she couldn't reconcile.

One Sunday evening, Lucas came home from school to find her seated at the table, surrounded by papers, pen clenched tightly in her hand. Worry was etched across her face.

Concerned, Lucas asked if she was okay. Amber didn't want to burden him, but being tired, her swollen eyes betrayed her. She pulled him into a hug and told him that she was just sorting out grown-up things. She forced a smile to shield him from her fear.

Lucas wandered off to watch TV, restless and bored, unaware of the weight his mother carried.

Amber, ever the devoted parent, thought about the future and the reality of Levi's absence from their lives. The thought terrified her.

She straightened her shoulders and said aloud, "Things will be fine." Turning back to Lucas, she added, "Let's forget the bills. Let's watch something funny together."

Lucas's laughter filled the room, and when he hugged her tightly, Amber drew strength from his joy.

CHAPTER 24
RESILIENCE IN THE RUINS

Amber often found herself reflecting on life after Levi, her thoughts always circling back to her son's future. The financial strain hit harder than she ever expected. Groceries, clothing, utility bills… every expense felt suffocating. The money Levi sent barely covered half of what Lucas needed. She knew she had to find a job.

Day after day, she sat at her computer, scanning job listings. Weeks passed, and hope slipped through her fingers.

Levi's unreliability pushed her to the edge one Monday afternoon. Slamming her hands onto the keyboard, Amber cursed his name under her breath. She had given up her dream of becoming a doctor for him. Now she was left to carry the financial burden alone.

Anger gave way to grief as memories of his broken promises flooded her.

"I told you I wanted to do my residency," she said aloud, voice cracking. "You kept pushing me off."

She buried her face in her hands, tears soaking her palms. Exhausted and alone, she refused to call Levi and beg. Slamming her laptop shut, she whispered fiercely, "I hate you, Levi."

Later, with Lucas still at school, Amber busied herself with small tasks, planning dinner, and sorting the bills, but the emptiness left by her divorce from Levi was crushing her. Looking up at the sky now, the late spring sunshine and the trees in full bloom didn't bring her any joy anymore, because her heart had turned to stone, weighed down by worry and uncertainty.

She didn't know how to find the energy, but she did know that she had to. For her son's sake, Amber thought about facing the day ahead. She drew on her own inner strength to teach him about being resilient.

Tears filled her eyes as she reached for her phone to call the one person with whom she didn't mind being completely vulnerable with—her mom.

Hesitant, because she was about to put herself in a very vulnerable spot, Amber blurted out "Mom" before dialing her mother's number. It was almost too difficult for her to ask for help, especially considering all the sacrifices her mother made to help her pursue her dream of becoming a doctor. When her mother answered, Amber was unable to speak, and her mother started to worry.

"Hello? Baby, is that you?"

The sound of her mother's voice completely broke Amber apart, and she started bawling down the phone, unable to stop.

"M-Mom. I can't. I won't be able to go through it all on my own anymore. I've tried, but it's just too much. I don't care who sees me crying in the street. My pain is getting too much to keep to myself, and only my mother can make me feel better. I need your help," Amber managed to say, and got the response she was counting on.

CHAPTER 25
SHELTER IN THE STORM

It took three days to go through everything, and each item pulled Amber backward in time, flooding her with memories as she and her son sorted through their belongings. Facing it all was emotionally brutal. It felt like walking through quicksand. She broke down in tears more than once, but she knew she couldn't afford to fall apart anymore, especially now that she was relying on her mother to be her anchor.

On a cloudy Saturday morning, Amber sat in the driveway, lost in thought, overwhelmed by the life she was about to leave behind. Relentless images of Levi's new life and of him moving forward with his new family crept into her mind, filling her with sorrow and uncertainty.

Just as the weight threatened to crush her, a small voice and a bright smile cut through the darkness. Lucas appeared at her side, still wearing his signature grin. He asked if he could carry his ball to their new house. Amber's eyes filled with tears, but she refused to dim his excitement.

"Of course, sweetheart," she said, keeping her voice light as she handed it to him.

Sensing his mother's sadness, Lucas stepped closer and wrapped his arms around her. His ball slipped from his hands and rolled away, thudding against the pavement. Each thud of that ball was a heart-stabber for Amber and made her think about what she had lost and was still losing.

Facing the fact that they'd be staying at his grandma's, Lucas asked his mother, "How long will we stay at Grandma's?"

Amber couldn't shake off the feeling of uncertainty about their situation, but she patted her hair as she looked at Lucas's face.

As Lucas looked up at her with wide, determined eyes, he said, "We'll be fine, Mom. I'll help you."

That was all it took to make Amber break down in tears. She held him in a tight hug and found herself struggling between guilt and pride. She had always been there for him, and now, he was trying to be there for her.

"My brave boy," she whispered, her voice trembling. "As long as we're together, we'll be okay."

As the moving truck came into view, rain began to fall. For the first time, Amber welcomed it. It felt like a cleansing—a beginning.

Soaked to the bone as they loaded the final boxes, mother

and son worked side by side, buoyed by each other's optimism. When they finally walked back to the car, Amber lifted her face to the rain-streaked sky and whispered a quiet, heartfelt "Thank you," feeling the weight on her chest ease, even if only slightly.

CHAPTER 26
A MOTHER'S WELCOME

When Amber pulled into her mother's driveway, she felt as though she had been granted a second chance. Her mother was already on the porch, her face lighting up the moment she saw them.

Lucas burst from the back seat, racing toward his grandmother and nearly knocking her over with the force of his hug. His laughter was contagious.

The yard was filled with kisses and warmth, and Amber's heart swelled. It felt as though she had never left. She was wrapped in a sense of belonging so strong it almost hurt.

"I missed you so much, Grandma!" Lucas shouted.

Amber smiled, but a new worry stirred beneath the surface. She was grateful to be home, but she didn't want to depend on her mother forever. This couldn't be more than a temporary refuge.

Lucas barely paused to breathe before his grandmother announced she had a surprise. His eyes widened, and he looked to Amber for confirmation.

"Don't look at me," Amber said with a laugh. "I don't know what it is."

Lucas cheered, begging to be taken inside. As they stepped through the door, Amber felt a deep sense of peace wash over her, wrapped in the joyful energy of her son, Lucas. Looking back at her relationship with Levi, Amber was coming to terms with the emptiness of financial security as a substitute for happiness, and realized that Lucas' happiness wasn't dependent on material possessions.

As she moved through the house, Amber was met by the dark brown sofa in her childhood home, a testament to her mother's fastidious nature. Unpleasant memories threatened to flood her, but a horn outside brought her back to the present. She yelled out to the movers who had arrived.

Familiar rain clouds had cleared, and the unloading went smoothly. Linda and Lucas handled lighter boxes together, working in perfect sync. In less than an hour, the truck was empty—a small victory that lifted Amber's mood.

Inside, the living room was stacked with boxes nearly reaching the ceiling. Lucas stared at them in awe.

"Is all this really ours?" he asked.

Linda pulled him into a hug. "You're one of the lucky ones."

Amber looked at the massive stack of boxes, reflecting on

all that she had managed to do for her son, and the financial weight of feeding him, dressing him, and sending him to college… all on her own.

CHAPTER 27
WHEN HOPE RETURNS

Each morning, Amber fell into the same routine. She scanned endless job listings and sent out her résumé to any position that might fit, even those that didn't feel right. Rejection followed rejection. As weeks turned into months, Amber started to feel desperate; her characteristically patient nature was beginning to fray.

Amber was not short-tempered, but more often than she liked, she snapped at Lucas. Linda, who had always been looking out for Amber, noticed the growing tension and decided it was time to intervene.

She said, "Amber, let's talk outside," and headed towards the door, expecting Amber to follow.

Out on the porch, Amber was weighed down by guilt and regret and trailed behind her mother, who was wearing the same look Amber knew her for—the one that meant something serious was coming.

"This isn't a joke, Amber. You really frightened Lucas."

Amber was crushed by her mother's response and dropped her defenses. She let her hair down and told her mother all about the difficulties she had been facing. Sending out thousands of applications and getting rejection mails... she couldn't bear the thought of being unable to take care of her family.

Amber was able to get a gentle smile on her face after hearing her mom's kind words of praise. Linda's words were so soothing that she gently brushed a tear from Amber's face. Linda lets Amber know that she'd always be there for her, and that she'd never have to figure out what it's like to be without her, because Levi didn't deserve her. Her mom's words gave her a renewed sense of self-confidence and made her feel like she wasn't blind to her own strengths all along.

They went inside and started cooking dinner for, and for the first time in weeks, Amber fell asleep soundly.

James stopped by Pluto Mall to buy a tie. As he turned down one of the aisles, he froze. Amber stood nearby, drifting through the clothing racks, unchanged in all the ways that mattered. Seeing her sent memories crashing through him, pulling him into the past.

She looked lighter and calmer somehow. The sight of her stirred something he had buried long ago. And in that moment, James made a decision. He needed to know how she was really doing. Because maybe, just maybe, fate wasn't finished with them yet.

CHAPTER 28
A CHANCE TO SHINE

When the call finally came from the person she had been waiting to hear from, Amber couldn't help but feel elated. After two long months, it was finally happening.

She babbled, "Tomorrow morning? What time? Absolutely, I'll be there. Thank you so much." She ran to her mom to share the news. Her voice was filled with relief and joy. After weeks of uncertainty, she could hardly believe this chance had come her way.

Her eyes met those of her son, Lucas, who stood in the doorway, caught between excitement and concern. He could tell something had shifted. Amber's radiant smile quickly reassured him.

"I have an interview," she announced.

Both of them sensed it. This was the beginning of something good.

Lucas rushed into her arms, hugging her tightly.

"You deserve it, Mom," he said with quiet certainty.

"Thank you, sweetheart," Amber replied, her heart full, before heading to her closet to find something impressive enough for the interview.

Thinking back on her goals, Amber had always wanted to be a doctor, but those long years of residency ahead of her made her take the job at the McGill Town Bank. It was a sensible choice, and a steppingstone to something else. Sleep didn't come easily. Thoughts of the interview circled endlessly until she finally drifted into a restless sleep. She woke up resolved. The idea of wearing a sharp black pantsuit and crisp white blouse felt right. A blue scarf she picked up on the way out added personality and confidence.

Giving herself a quiet pep talk, Amber stepped out the door, fortified and ready to show who she truly was.

The imposing structure of McGill Town Bank took her breath away—its fusion of baroque and art nouveau styles. Amber pictured herself thriving in this setting. A kindly-voiced woman called out her name. She turned to see Valerie Morgan. Her charming look and cascading dark hair in vogue caused Amber to feel at ease and more assured about the direction her life was headed.

"Have a seat," Valerie said. "I'll be running the interview. I think we might have something in common. I was going to be a doctor once, too. Then life took me in a different direction."

The interview flowed easily. As it ended, Amber felt something she hadn't felt in a long time. Hope.

CHAPTER 29
THE STRENGTH WITHIN

After the interview, Amber could do nothing but wait. Three agonizing days passed before she finally got the call.

"Congratulations, Amber," Valerie said brightly. "You're part of the team."

Amber's jaw dropped. Linda, sitting nearby, smiled knowingly.

As Valerie outlined Amber's schedule and start date, gratitude flooded her. She threw her arms around her mother, overwhelmed. This job changed everything.

She started the following Monday. She worked 9 to 5, Monday to Friday. She got to the office right on time and always wore a smile. People queued up to ask her for help to sort out their banking, and Amber took pride in helping those in need. The happiness of her son Lucas, especially, gave her a deep sense of pride. She was not in a very financially stable position but was happy to have a job. Coming out of a challenging period in her life, she was still experiencing a bit of roughness.

Three months later, everything changed. Amber walked into the house and found Lucas pale and unsteady. His eyes were dull; his speech was slow. She dropped to her knees in front of him.

"What's wrong, sweetheart?"

Linda appeared from the kitchen, holding peppermint tea. "He's been like this for ten minutes," she said. "I was just about to call you."

Linda started speculating that he had probably eaten something that his digestive system couldn't tolerate. Amber was concerned about how to help him feel better. She asked him gently,

"Honey, where does it hurt?" Lucas couldn't speak, so he pointed to his stomach, grimacing.

Amber's anxiety went off the charts, and she thought he might be in serious trouble. When his eyes rolled back, she didn't hesitate.

"That's it. I'm calling an ambulance."

"For a stomachache?" Linda asked, startled.

Amber shook her head. "I'm not risking it."

CHAPTER 30
FIERCE IN THE FIRE

Amber tore through the emergency department, barely aware of the stares she drew. She ran past partitions and curtained bays, calling his name. Brushing away fresh tears and checking the monitors, she felt better when she saw the steady readings, but was revolted by the sight of the IV in his arm. She tried to follow the gurney, grabbing its side, but a nurse blocked her path to the ICU.

"Ma'am, you can't go in there."

The nurse wouldn't listen to Amber's frantic plea.

"We need to run some tests and will fill you in as soon as we can, but for now, you need to calm down," she said. "You're not doing Lucas any favors like this."

Amber's heart was racing away, but she took a deep breath, understanding that the nurse was right. She agreed to wait.

"I'll wait here. Please, just tell me as soon as you know anything." The nurse's gentle tone calmed her down a bit.

Amber started pacing up and down the corridors, spiraling through all sorts of terrible thoughts, none of which could calm her down because she believed Lucas was suffering. She couldn't do anything to stop it.

She suddenly bumped into someone, apologized, and then froze when she looked up to see the face of the person she least wanted to see—Levi. His eyes were blazing in a way she hadn't seen before. Levi ran over to the intensive care unit and asked for Lucas. Being an experienced doctor, Amber trusted in his ability to navigate the hospital system without any issues. But what was he doing here in a white coat and ID badge, pretending to be a regular employee?

"What are you doing here, Levi, and why are you at this hospital?" she asked, her voice trembling with fear and anger. But he didn't even give her a second look, being completely fixated on his son.

"What happened to him? What did you do to my son?" he barked, which didn't sit well with Amber.

"Your son? Funny how he's suddenly yours now," Amber shot back. "He was ours, then mine when you left… and now he's yours again?"

Levi bristled, claiming he had supported them, and paid what he could.

"That doesn't even cover the basics," Amber said coldly. "Don't pretend you're not responsible."

She turned to leave. He grabbed her arm.

"Let go of me," she warned. "I'll call security."

Something in her voice cut through him. Levi released her as if burned.

CHAPTER 31
ROOTS OF HOPE

Amber recoiled as Levi released her, her anger barely contained. Before either of them could speak, a nurse appeared, guiding Lucas through the swinging doors on a hospital bed. Color had returned to his cheeks, and he looked much improved.

"It was an allergic reaction," the attending doctor explained, glancing between the parents. "Something he ate. Nothing too severe. He probably consumed something at school or—"

The doctor's words trailed off as Amber rushed to Lucas's side. Relief flooded her as she wrapped her arms around her son.

"Are you all right, sweetheart?" she asked, her voice trembling as she searched his face.

Lucas nodded slowly. As his eyes drifted past her, he

noticed Levi standing behind her. Levi remained motionless, taking in the sight of his recovering son. Amber's earlier accusations echoed in his mind. No matter how hard he tried to ignore them, he couldn't escape the truth. He had prioritized his new family, leaving his son behind, just as Amber had said.

Guilt gnawed at him, and he realized how unnatural it now felt to stand there as a present father. Still, he forced a weak smile and stepped forward.

"Hey, champ. How're you feeling?"

Amber shifted aside to let Levi approach. She refused to let her anger surface in front of Lucas. This wasn't the moment for conflict. She watched with folded arms as father and son shared a brief, awkward exchange.

After a few minutes, Amber leaned in gently. "Ready to go home?"

Lucas nodded, exhaustion in his voice. "Yeah. I want to leave. Hospitals scare me."

His eyes flicked around the room, and Amber could tell that both the hospital and Levi unsettled him.

"We'll be home soon, love," she promised. "Just a little longer."

A nurse wheeled Lucas into a nearby room to complete the discharge paperwork, leaving Levi and Amber alone.

"You never told me he had allergies," Levi said sharply, frustration etched across his face.

Amber, drained and unwilling to argue, replied through clenched teeth. "I didn't know. And honestly, why would you care? You were hardly ever around."

She turned away, but Levi's voice stopped her. "All I care about right now is my son," he said. "Whether you believe it or not."

Amber rolled her eyes and walked toward the nurses' station to sign the paperwork and take Lucas home.

Seeing Levi had reopened old wounds, but she pushed the thoughts aside. Her focus was on Lucas and his recovery. She had no energy for anything else.

That evening, Amber found her son sprawled across the living room floor, surrounded by school projects and scattered papers, chatting away to himself. She paused in the doorway as his words drifted toward her.

"One day, I'm going to be rich," Lucas declared, his voice full of conviction. "I'll buy Mom a big house, like a castle, with a pool. And a huge garden with flowers and trees." He nodded seriously. "Mom loves flowers. She deserves the best. She works so hard for me."

Amber felt pride swell in her chest. Linda approached from behind, but Amber gently stopped her.

"Let him have this moment, Mom," she whispered, brushing away a tear. "He already dreams so big."

The two women stood quietly, watching as Lucas continued.

"I need to figure out how to make money," he said. "I want to take charge and be the man of the house."

He tapped his chin thoughtfully, then brightened. "What if I sell my toys? And the clothes I don't need?" He nodded eagerly. "I could go around the neighborhood. No equipment needed. What about a yard sale?"

His eyes lit up. "I'll make flyers and knock on every door!" he laughed, completely satisfied with his plan.

Linda wiped away tears of pride. Amber smiled, her heart overflowing.

"That boy is going to change the world someday," Linda whispered.

Amber knew she was right. He would.

CHAPTER 32
AMBER'S LITTLE ENTREPRENEUR

The next morning, Amber sat at the breakfast table with her son, eager to encourage his new venture.

"So," she said lightly, smiling, "how are preparations for the yard sale coming along? Is there anything I can do to help?"

Lucas froze, eyes wide, stunned that his mother already knew. Then, his face broke into a grin. Without hesitation, he jumped up and wrapped Amber in a tight hug.

Laughter filled the kitchen. In that moment, Amber felt whole. Her son's love was everything.

"Thanks, Mom! You're the best!" Lucas cheered.

Amber hugged him back, pride swelling. Despite everything with Levi, she knew she had all she truly needed right here.

Over the next few days, Lucas gathered his old clothes and

even convinced his grandmother to take him thrifting to find more items to resell. He made his own signs, and to everyone's amazement, earned over a hundred dollars on the first day.

Amber watched from the porch as neighbors stopped by and customers returned. The next day, Lucas made three hundred dollars, leaving Amber stunned that her son might soon be earning more than she was.

As the evening settled, Lucas counted his earnings carefully. Amber stepped inside to give him space.

"Four hundred dollars!" he exclaimed, eyes wide. "I can buy you something special, Mom. Or give you all of it. You deserve it!"

He dropped to his knees beside her, spreading the bills across the floor. "I want to buy you a present. You've worked so hard since Dad left."

Amber shook her head gently. "No way. That money is yours. You earned it."

"But I want to!" Lucas insisted. "You always buy things for me. Why can't I do the same for you? We finally have enough."

Amber smiled softly. "Money doesn't just appear out of nowhere. You should save it for when you really need something. I'm okay, I promise."

Lucas frowned, thinking. Then he said quietly, "I don't want the money. From now on, everything I have is yours."

He handed her the cash reverently. "One day, I'll be a multi-millionaire and buy you everything you want. I'll take care of you."

Then he added, "When I'm the man of the house, I'll start a real business. One that helps people."

Tears filled Amber's eyes. She knelt and pulled him into a hug.

"That's a beautiful dream," she said softly. "But remember, money isn't everything. What matters most is that we stick together and treat each other with kindness."

Lucas nodded, though he didn't fully understand. "I just want to help you," he said.

Amber kissed the top of his head. "I love your big dreams. But don't rush growing up. You're still my little boy."

Even so, the determination in his eyes was unmistakable.

For months, Lucas set up yard sales every weekend while Amber worked extra shifts. She never intended to live with Linda forever. Her goal was to buy a place of her own, which meant long hours and overtime.

Still, money slipped through her fingers. Bills, groceries, clothes, school supplies. Everything took priority.

"These prices are ridiculous," Amber muttered during a grocery run.

Linda nodded. "Just look at the cost of eggs."

Amber sighed. "It shouldn't cost this much to live."

As they approached the checkout, Amber noticed a sign taped to the wall: Help Wanted.

Her face brightened. "It's part-time," she said. "Should I apply? I need the extra money, but I won't be home as much."

She glanced at Lucas. "What do you think? Could you help out more?"

Linda smiled warmly. "Of course. I'll help however you need."

Relief washed over Amber as she hugged her mother. "Thank you. I knew I could count on you."

Ignoring the curious looks around them, she nodded. "I know. Let's pay for these groceries."

Amber pocketed the flyer. She knew she could do this.

For Lucas, she would do anything.

CHAPTER 33
DREAMS AFTER DARK

Three days later, Amber received a call inviting her to an interview. She attended that same day, aced it, and was offered the job immediately. The news filled her with excitement, even though she knew the shifts would run late into the evening.

That night, Amber arrived home to find her son once again sprawled across the living room floor. She set down her bag, lifted her arms in triumph, and announced with a wide smile, "I got the job!"

Lucas leaped up, shouting with joy, and rushed to embrace her.

"That's amazing, Mom!" he exclaimed. "You're the best mom ever!"

Amber's heart overflowed with happiness. She gently pulled back, laughing as she looked him in the eye.

"Pretty cool, huh?" she said. "Maybe now we can save up for a place of our own. What do you think?"

Lucas's eyes widened. "A house where we each get our own room?"

Amber nodded, eager to encourage the dream. But she noticed a flicker of worry cross his face.

"Mom… this is awesome, but aren't you working too much?" he asked softly. "I don't want you to get tired."

Amber knew he wasn't wrong, but she was determined to push forward for his sake. She smiled softly and reassured him, "I'll be fine, I promise. You need to focus on your schoolwork. Leave the adult stuff to me, okay?"

Lucas hesitated, but the resolve in his mother's eyes convinced him. He nodded, his voice barely above a whisper. "Okay, Mom."

They shared another embrace while Linda watched from the doorway. She understood Amber's struggle; she had faced similar challenges herself, but she knew Amber's journey was her own.

Around the same time, Cooper, James' trusted assistant, entered the grand house as instructed. He carried a thick folder packed with photographs, receipts, notes, and carefully compiled records documenting Amber and her son's daily lives. James had demanded every detail.

Cooper dropped the file onto the kitchen island. James immediately set aside his coffee. Dressed in crisp white and clearly prepared for a day of golf with his affluent peers, he forgot all about his plans and sat down.

"It's all here, sir. Everything you asked for," Cooper said.

James flipped through the stack, grimacing. "Can't you just give me the highlights? I don't have time to read all this right now."

Cooper stifled a sigh. If the situation justified surveillance, James could spare a few minutes. Still, he complied.

"She's a good person, completely devoted to her son. But she's stretched thin. She works two jobs—a full-time position at a bank and part-time shifts at a grocery store. She leaves before sunrise and gets home late. Every day is the same routine."

He paused before continuing. "The kid runs yard sales every weekend outside his grandmother's place. He works hard, boss. It's impressive, but honestly… it's heartbreaking. It's not normal for a child to shoulder that kind of responsibility. They're barely keeping afloat, but she's a fighter."

James listened in silence, his coffee suddenly bitter. Each word weighed heavier than the last.

"Want more detail?" Cooper asked. "I can go deeper, but that's the gist."

James didn't respond right away. He pictured Amber as she had been in college. Bright. Energetic. Always smiling. He had imagined a very different life for her.

"That's not right," James said finally. "We need to do something."

Cooper raised an eyebrow. "You want me to just hand her some cash?"

James shook his head sharply. "No. It needs to be discreet."

Cooper hesitated. "Then maybe you should reach out yourself. You have history."

James shot him a hard look. "Absolutely not. You have no idea what happened between us."

Cooper immediately backed off. "Understood. Didn't mean to cross a line."

"You can go," James said curtly.

Once Cooper left, James sank onto the white leather sofa, file in hand, and began to sift through the documents. The photographs drew him in. He studied each one carefully, hardly daring to breathe.

Amber's beauty hadn't faded, even after all these years. The woman in the pictures was unmistakably the same Amber he'd known at university. Her spirit was still visible, though her features now bore the marks of hardship, and her eyes had lost some of their old brightness. James's heart raced, even in her absence.

"Amber. Why did it have to turn out this way?" he murmured, pressing one of the photos gently to his cheek.

CHAPTER 34
CAN'T STOP THINKING ABOUT YOU

James had been thinking nonstop about how to help Amber and her son. By the end of the week, he had a plan. He asked Cooper to accompany him to Lucas's yard sale, knowing Amber would be at work. It would give him the chance to meet the boy alone.

On Saturday morning, they drove to the address. The front yard was lined with folding tables piled high with books, toys, and old electronics. Lucas stood behind the tables, bright-eyed and confident, managing the sale with impressive authority.

"Hello there," James said, approaching. "How's business?"

Lucas looked up and grinned. "Hello, sir. Business is thriving."

James smiled, immediately charmed. This child was articulate, confident, and more composed than many adults.

"I came to buy everything you have," James said calmly, "but only if you agree to one condition."

Lucas raised an eyebrow. "Everything? As long as the condition isn't illegal."

James laughed. "Nothing illegal. You're an impressive young man."

"All right," Lucas said thoughtfully. "Tell me the condition."

James glanced at Cooper, struck by the thought that this boy should have been his son.

"I'll give you five hundred thousand dollars for everything here," James said, "on one condition. You focus on school, do your best, and when you're finished, come work for my company. And most importantly, always take care of your mom."

Lucas's eyes widened. "Five hundred thousand? Sir, my things aren't worth that much. I can't take your money."

James smiled. "You could use it to help your mom. Maybe buy her a house."

Lucas hesitated, then nodded eagerly. "If I agree, could we buy her a house today? She's working late. She has two jobs."

"Absolutely," James said.

He turned to Cooper. "Pack everything."

Then to Lucas, he said, "Call your grandmother. Give her Cooper's number. He'll take you to the mall. Have her speak to him so she knows you're safe."

Cooper handed over his ID. Lucas sent a photo to his grandmother and handed over the phone. James had already arranged the rest. His real estate agent met them at a foreclosed property valued at four hundred thousand dollars, available for three hundred thousand.

The house looked like a castle. Lucas stared in awe. "Sir... can I really buy this for my mom?"

James nodded. "If you want it, it's yours."

"Yes!" Lucas exclaimed.

James arranged for the title to be placed in Amber's and Lucas's names.

Lucas paused. "Can we add my grandma's name, too?"

The realtor updated the paperwork accordingly.

"I have to get home before Mom does," Lucas said anxiously.

James smiled. "You still have two hundred thousand left. When you get home, ask your mom for her account number. I'll wire the rest. I keep my promises."

Lucas shook his hand. "Thank you, sir. I promise I'll do well in school and work for you one day."

He hesitated, then whispered with a mischievous grin, "My mom is single. Would you like to meet her?"

James chuckled. "Let's keep this between us for now. But yes. I would."

As Lucas left, James felt something unfamiliar settle in his chest. Hope.

CHAPTER 35
A DEAL FOR THE FUTURE

Lucas arrived home before his mother and grandmother, exactly as he'd planned.

When Amber finally walked through the door, she was so exhausted from her long shifts that she barely managed a tired smile before collapsing onto the couch. Lucas rushed to her side and wrapped her in a tight hug.

"Mom, I love you," he said.

Half-asleep, Amber smiled. "I love you more."

Just before she drifted off, Lucas asked casually, "Mom, what's your bank account number?"

Amber frowned, confused, but too tired to question him. She reached into her bag, pulled out her checkbook, and handed it over.

"Here," she mumbled, already dozing.

Lucas quickly snapped a photo of the account numbers

and texted it to Cooper. Moments later, a confirmation notification: The deposit had gone through. Lucas quietly slipped the checkbook back into her bag.

The next morning, Amber was making breakfast when Lucas bounded into the kitchen, showering her with kisses and hugs.

"Good morning, Mom!"

She smiled sleepily. "Good morning, my lovely son."

Grinning from ear to ear, Lucas announced, "I have a gift for you. Check your bank account."

Curious, Amber picked up her phone and opened her banking app. Her breath caught when she saw the balance.

Two hundred thousand dollars.

"Lucas," she gasped, panic surging, "what did you do? Where did this money come from? Oh my gosh, we're going to be in trouble. We have to return this right now."

Before Lucas could explain, Amber grabbed his hand and rushed him out the door, determined to get answers.

At the bank, a representative listened carefully as Amber spilled out the story. "My son told me to check my account, and now there's all this money. He says it's a gift."

The representative turned to Lucas. "Where did you get this money?"

Lucas finally had his chance. "I sold my yard sale items to a man for five hundred thousand dollars."

Amber and the bank representative stared at him in disbelief. "Five hundred thousand?" they echoed.

Lucas nodded calmly. "Yes. I also bought a house for my mom that day. Here's the paperwork."

He handed over the title documents.

The bank representative examined them closely, then nodded. "These are legitimate."

Lucas produced a business card. "This is Mr. Cooper and his friend. You can call them to confirm."

The bank manager placed the call. Cooper verified everything and explained that the funds had come directly from the title company. He then asked to speak with Amber.

"Hello, Mr. Cooper," Amber said, still stunned. "Why did you give my son so much money?"

"I didn't give him anything," Cooper replied gently. "He earned it. We negotiated. You should be proud of him."

James, listening quietly on the other end, chuckled.

Cooper understood exactly why James had insisted on keeping his involvement hidden. Amber would have returned the money without hesitation.

Amber sat in stunned silence, struggling to grasp that her son had accomplished what she had worked toward for decades. Tears filled her eyes as she turned to Lucas.

"I'm so sorry, sweetheart. Please forgive me for not trusting you. I was scared."

Lucas hugged her tightly, tears streaming down his face. "You don't need to apologize, Mom. I love you. Let's go home, okay?"

Amber nodded.

On the way, Lucas asked shyly, "Can we see the house I bought for you first?"

When they arrived, Amber was speechless. The house was beautiful. She hugged Lucas fiercely. "Thank you. You are my heart."

"You can quit your part-time job now," Lucas said softly. "I want to spend more time with you."

That very day, Amber resigned from her grocery store job. She, Lucas, and Linda moved into their new home together. Linda rented out her own house temporarily.

Amber's life had changed beyond anything she could have imagined, all because of her son's heart, integrity, and a little help from unexpected friends.

CHAPTER 36
A STEP TOO LATE

The mere thought of being near Amber again stirred a restless wave of emotion inside James. He exhaled slowly, sinking deeper into the sofa as his eyes scanned the scattered photos and documents before him. Lucas looked bright and happy in the images, and the realization that, under different circumstances, he might have been the boy's father cut him deeply.

That night, James lay awake on the couch, unable to calm his thoughts. His heart urged him to reconnect with Amber, but his mind warned him of how complicated that would be.

Days turned into weeks. Regret haunted him during the day, and restless dreams followed him at night. He knew he couldn't stay frozen forever.

Then, one late Saturday afternoon, everything shifted. James wandered through the city, hoping the noise and movement would drown out his thoughts. Only Cooper walked beside him.

He stopped abruptly, his attention drawn to a softly lit restaurant. Flowers adorned the tables inside, casting a warm glow. And there she was.

Amber sat alone, wearing a crisp white blouse, her dark hair cascading over her shoulders. The gentle curve of her smile stole his breath. James swallowed hard.

"Boss?" Cooper nudged him.

"She's stunning," James murmured.

"Go talk to her," Cooper urged.

James tugged at his collar, feeling flushed, anxiety prickling across his skin.

"What are you waiting for? She's right there. Just say hello, I'm sure she'll be glad to see you after all this time," Cooper pressed, his encouragement igniting a flicker of hope in James.

"Do you really think so?" James asked, searching Cooper's face for reassurance.

Cooper smiled and nodded, boosting his confidence.

James straightened his jacket, took a deep breath, and, rehearsing what he might say after all these years, crossed the street and pushed open the restaurant door. With each step across the marble floor, memories of their past surged. Then a man approached Amber's table.

She stood and leaned in, pressing a kiss to his cheek. James froze.

What he didn't know was that the kiss was accidental. It

was a result of Amber's heavy wine drinking that afternoon. The sight struck James like a sudden blow.

He froze, stunned, unable to comprehend what he was witnessing. There was no betrayal—too much time had passed—but the pain of lost opportunities overwhelmed him. Breathless, James turned and hurried out of the restaurant, his vision blurring.

Cooper hurried after him. "What happened? Did you talk to her?"

James said nothing.

Cooper glanced back and saw Amber laughing with the man. Understanding dawned. "Damn it."

When James reached the car, he climbed inside and stared straight ahead.

"Where to?" Cooper asked quietly.

James didn't answer.

All he wanted was distance from the regret, from the jealousy, from the crushing weight of what might have been.

In a charming restaurant filled with rich aromas and soft melodies, Amber drank wine a little too freely.

The chosen bottle warmed her from the inside out, tinting her cheeks pink and widening her smile. When her glass was empty, she signaled the waiter for another pour.

She was dining alone that late afternoon, indulging in a rare moment of self-care at her mother's insistence.

Linda had promised to stay home with Lucas, baking cookies and watching movies, practically pushing Amber out the door.

"Meet a friend or enjoy some 'me' time," her mother had said. "You deserve it. Go somewhere nice."

With every sip, Amber thought her mother had been right. This small escape was exactly what she needed. The divorce had shattered her. The comforts of married life were gone, replaced by financial strain and constant uncertainty about her and her son's future.

Then, unexpectedly, her young son had gifted her a house and deposited $200,000 into her bank account. For the first time in a while, she could breathe.

She began humming along to the music playing in the background, deciding it was the perfect moment to visit the restroom. Her sparkling blue eyes shone brightly, and though her balance wavered slightly, she felt light and free. As she edged from her seat without looking up, she collided with something solid.

Startled, she froze. Then, the scent of a captivating cologne settled her nerves. She looked up and found herself face to face with a handsome stranger passing her table. Her eyes lit up. Without thinking, Amber leaned in and kissed him. It was something she would never normally do, but the wine and her sudden sense of freedom had lifted her into a near-euphoric haze.

Almost immediately, his arms wrapped around her waist. The hold was firm, grounding, and unexpectedly comforting.

SELECTING THE WRONG LOVE

Though the kiss lasted only seconds, it stretched endlessly in her mind. The mix of wine, adrenaline, and electric chemistry created an intoxicating rush.

"I'm sorry," the man murmured.

Amber barely registered the words. She noticed his slicked-back hair and thought he looked like he'd stepped straight out of a magazine, which made her smile.

Neither of them moved. It felt as though the restaurant had disappeared, leaving only the two of them suspended in a quiet bubble.

Too tipsy to feel embarrassed, Amber's thoughts wandered. Her gaze drifted back to his lips. On impulse, she leaned in again and stole another kiss. This one was softer, deeper, and edged with yearning. A quiet moan escaped her before she could stop herself.

Despite the crowded room, Amber felt no shame. When they finally parted, her open, unguarded expression made him smile. Then she blurted out, husky and unfiltered, "Marry me!"

The man stared at her, stunned by her beauty and audacity. Was she joking? Or completely out of her mind?

"What?" he asked at last, his hands falling from her waist as reality caught up with her. Amber giggled and repeated, "Marry me…"

Realizing how ridiculous she must sound, she added more softly, "Don't mind me. I'm a little tipsy. Forget I said anything."

It felt like his cue to walk away. Instead, his eyes lingered, tracing the elegant line of her figure, the tempting neckline of her blouse, the black pants hugging her curves.

She looked unreal. Like a dream.

"How could I forget a kiss like that?" he said.

His response emboldened her. Turning back to him, she teased, "So, will you marry me today?"

Her voice wavered just slightly. He looked even more unsteady than she felt.

"Answer me," she pressed. "Will you marry me today?"

He hesitated, then finally said, "I'll marry you if you promise to kiss me like that every day for the rest of my life."

Amber's eyes widened. She could not believe this playful fantasy was continuing. Strangers did not get married after one accidental kiss. At least, not in real life.

She laughed and slid back into her seat. The restroom could wait.

"Deal," she said, giggling again.

Her skin tingled under his gaze, her mind buzzing with excitement. She felt alive, reckless, and young. Like anything was possible again. He sat across from her, chuckling as he reached for her hand. He held it a moment longer than necessary, studying her face.

"I'm Amber," she said, smiling and extending her hand properly this time.

"I'm Rian Ekinley," he replied. "Nice to meet you, my wife."

At the word *wife*, Amber sprang to her feet and dropped into the seat beside him.

Without hesitation, she kissed him again, fierce and playfully.

"Let's go get married right now," she declared loudly. "He called me his wife. I am his wife!"

She grabbed Rian's hand, tugging him up. "Come on. Let's do this. Let's get married now."

Rian stood frozen, speechless. And somewhere beyond the wine, the laughter, and the reckless thrill of the moment, the shadows of the past began to stir.

WILL LEVI'S OBSESSION PUSH HIM TO REVEAL THE SECRET he's kept buried?

Will Amber risk reopening old wounds or finally break free once and for all?

Can Amber seize the love and freedom she longs for…or is the darkness about to consume her completely?

The chapter closes here, but the story is only beginning. And what comes next will be far more dangerous.

Get your copy today of book two in this series and find out what happens next!
Selecting My Soulmate
Book 2 of the LoveWade Tale Series
Available June 18, 2026

About the Authors E. Masson and Julie G. Henry

E. Masson and Julie G. Henry are indie authors who craft heartfelt romance stories.

With pens full of dreams and hearts full of passion, they create tales of love and resilience that resonate deeply with readers.

From whirlwind romances to slow burn love stories, their novels are infused with warmth, emotion, and a touch of magic, making them impossible to put down. Each character is carefully brought to life, and every setting is designed to transport readers into enchanting new worlds.

Storytelling has always been a shared love for E. Masson and Julie G. Henry, and turning that passion into a writing career has allowed them to create novels that both entertain and move readers.

With over 5,000 Kindle downloads, E. Masson's debut novel has already captured the hearts of readers, who eagerly ask for more.

When she isn't writing, E. Masson enjoys exploring new places and discovering inspiration in the beauty of everyday life.

She believes every story holds the power to heal and uplift, a belief that shines through in each of her books.

Step into E. Masson's world of storytelling and fall in love with stories that linger long after the last page.

Visit: www.AuthoremMasson.com

Contact the author: https://www.authoremasson.com/pages/contact

amazon.com/author/emassonbooks

bookbub.com/authors/e-masson

Also by E. Masson and Julie G. Henry

The Quadrillionaire Brothers

Empire of Billions

Symphony of a Heart in Pieces

In Sickness and Health:

A Husband's Eternal Vow

The LoveWade Tale

Selecting the Wrong Love

Selecting My Soulmate

A Note from the Author

Hello, Lovely Readers,

It would be so fantastic if you could take a moment to leave a review on Amazon, Bookbub, and Goodreads . Your feedback really helps other readers discover my work. Thank you in advance for your support. I truly appreciate every single one of you!

Love,
E. Masson & Julie G. Henry

Printed in Dunstable, United Kingdom